THE BLEEDING HORSE
AND OTHER GHOST STORIES

THE BLEEDING HORSE
AND OTHER GHOST STORIES

BRIAN J. SHOWERS
Illustrated by Duane Spurlock

MERCIER PRESS
WHAT YOU NEED TO READ

MERCIER PRESS
Cork
www.mercierpress.ie

Trade enquiries to CMD Distribution
55A Spruce Avenue, Stillorgan Industrial Park,
Blackrock, County Dublin.

Extracts from Kilpatrick's *Phantoms and Apparitions of South Dublin* and the
Irish Classics edition of *Father Corrigan's Diary* used with permission from
the publishers.

ISBN: 978 1 85635 578 0

10 9 8 7 6 5 4 3 2 1

In memory of Deirdre Kelly, whose scholarship haunts this book's every
page. And for Anna-Lena Yngve, who worked just as hard for this book
as I did.

A CIP record for this title is available from the British Library

arts
council
chomhairle
ealaíon   Mercier Press receives financial assistance from the Arts
             Council/An Chomhairle Ealaíon

Printed and bound by J.H. Haynes & Co. Ltd, Sparkford

'Local history can, I believe, play a very important social role in helping to counter that sense of alienation which so often plagues our modern society. A sense of significance of local buildings, of local traditions ... all such factors emerge from the story of local history.'

Kevin B. Nowlan,
Introduction to *Four Roads to Dublin*

'Take my word for it, there is no such thing as an ancient village, especially if it has seen better days, un-illustrated by its legends of terror. You may as well expect to find decayed cheese without mites, or an old house without rats, as an antique and dilapidated town without an authentic population of goblins.'

Joseph Sheridan Le Fanu,
Ghost Stories of Chapelizod

Scribo namque quae neque vidi, neque ipse passus sum, aut ab aliis accepi, magis autem quae omnino non sunt neque fieri potuerunt. Quare in haec incidunt, nullatenus credere.

Lucianus Samosatensis
Veræ Historiæ

Contents

Introduction

The folkloric ghost story has a long, chequered history ranging at least as far back as mythology will trace, through the Roman Houses of Hades, to such present-day collectors of urban legends as Jan Harold Brunvand. Few of those printed leave lasting impressions, being little more than bare records of events with no care taken to: delineate the characters involved (either natural or supernatural); place the events within their familial, geographical, historical or wider folkloric/mythological contexts; or even describe the events with sufficient finesse to lend them atmosphere and impact. The story-teller of old could make up for what looked bare on the page by reshaping his tales with details from each new site visited and long practice at creating dramatic effects through voice, gesture and expression.

Of the hundreds of ghost stories and weird events culled from folklore for the printed page over the centuries, those that have proved most memorable have been the relatively few tales on which the author has imposed a shape, recreated a context and at least hinted at a purpose. A convincing ghost story could be written about the spectre of Myrtilus haunting the stadium at Olympia following his betrayal and murder by Pelops, but the full impact of the story requires the author's deployment of all those elements noted as missing from the majority of recorded folkloric ghost stories, including, in this case, references to the crimes of Pelops' father, Tantalus, and a veritable litany of succeeding tragedies that ultimately led to the destruction of Troy, the murder of Pelops' grandson Agamemnon at the hands of another grandson, Aegisthus, and the madness of Agamemnon's surviving children. Few ghost stories have such a broad scope as this, yet the successful ghost story based on folklore always explores or hints at something – whether event, emotion or a fierce combination of the two – greater than the mere recital of details can ever hope to encompass.

We encounter this most frequently in myth, but we also see it in tragedy, ballad, verse and the more literary forms of the ghost story which started to appear in the nineteenth century. The details of the hauntings in such ballads as 'William and Marjorie', 'The Wife of Usher's Well' and 'The Unquiet Grave' are interesting enough, but what makes us remember them so fondly and so clearly is their depth of longing and their sense of place – they make us recognise that these are not quaint events purported to have taken place among a group of superstitious nonentities in the remote past, but tragedies with significant repercussions affecting real people in a specific place and time. As the Age of Enlightenment gave way to Sensibility and thence to the Romantic movement, authors, searching for an art that eschewed the artificiality and preciosity of the eighteenth century in favour of greater intensity and a closer contact between free men and sublime nature, enriched both their verse and their prose through the influence of the folk tale and the ballad. This fertilising influence has had a profound effect on authors as diverse as William Wordsworth, Samuel Taylor Coleridge, Sir Walter Scott, James Hogg, Johann Wolfgang von Goethe, Göttfried August Bürger, Ludwig Tieck and others.

By the time Joseph Sheridan Le Fanu began publishing his first folklore-based ghost stories in the *Dublin University Magazine* in 1838, the folk tale, the local legend and the ballad had become grist for the literary mill. It must be borne in mind that Le Fanu and his brother William assiduously researched the folkways of the areas in which they lived, to the extent that their expertise was relied upon by the folklorists Samuel Carter Hall and Anna Maria Hall when compiling the immense three-volume guidebook to Ireland they published between 1841 and 1843. What sets Le Fanu apart from a great many of his contemporaries in this endeavour is his attempt to capture as closely as possible the inflexions of a local storyteller, the scenic grandeur or peculiarities of the place in which events occurred, and the precise speech patterns and personalities of the individuals involved. At the same time he would pace events with the utmost precision, imparting the proper atmospheric effects to each event and location, and injecting a sense that events described are mere fragments of a larger and more ominous pattern that mortal man might never fully comprehend. He demonstrated this artful melding of seemingly naïve material and narrators with extreme sophistication throughout his literary career, from the earliest of the Father Purcell tales in 1838 to 'Laura Silver Bell' and 'Dickon the Devil' published the year before his death in 1873. And the more closely he ties them to a particular time and place, the more powerful they are. These are aspects of his supernatural fiction that also inform and interpenetrate those works not directly influenced by folklore.

Of particular interest here are two sets of linked stories Le Fanu published almost twenty years apart: 'Ghost Stories of Chapelizod' (*Dublin University Magazine*, January 1851) and 'Stories of Lough Guir' (*All the Year Round*, 23 April 1870). Each story in each set not only works independently, but also gains strength from shared motifs that add resonance to its fellows. Le Fanu wishes to remind us that these supernatural events do not occur in isolation, but are manifestations of a vaster spiritual world impinging upon our natural one and ever ready to break through.

Readers of the present collection may find it disquieting that Mr Showers has allowed similar motifs to echo within these pages, to chilling effect. When, for instance, a horse similar to that described in the first story appears in a later tale under different circumstances, what are we to make of it? And if a corpse is found in an unexpected place with its mouth stuffed with lavender, what should we conclude about a man in a later story who insists upon the presence of lavender whenever alone? These details, among others, summon a whole host of uncomfortable surmises, surmises which the narrator of the stories seems all too willing to overlook.

Rathmines may not be separated by a great physical distance from Le Fanu's Chapelizod, but it would be comforting to believe that the intervening century and a half had at least dimmed, if not entirely obscured, the chillier implications Le Fanu revealed in the *rapprochement* between his region and its damning past. Showers' careful marshalling of the facts from diverse sources and a cloud of witnesses proves otherwise. These ghost stories of Rathmines, often deceptively light in tone, are full of the kinds of twists and turns that make safety look illusory, shrink the distance between passive reader and active witness, and bring the recurrent past ever before our eyes.

Jim Rockhill
Dowagiac, Michigan
October 2007

A Note To The Reader

I should probably take this opportunity to inform the readers of this book that my introduction, though true as far as it goes, is also a trifle disingenuous. Brian J. Showers and I have never met in person, but have been carrying on a lively correspondence via internet and post since Barbara Roden of the Ghost Story Society sent me for review and comment an early draft of what would later become the Le Fanu chapter of his *Literary Walking Tours of Gothic Dublin* (Nonsuch Ireland, 2006). To my delight Brian was as enamoured of Le Fanu's work as I was, and had been doing a considerable amount of research into the urban geography in which the man lived and worked.

Although an amiable correspondent and generous with the fruits of his research, Brian seems by nature a private person. Rarely has he mentioned personal matters, and on those occasions early in our correspondence when he offered a few details of his life and I responded as if more details were forthcoming, he became aloof, and on one occasion did not respond at all for several days. Over the years the sum of what I have learned about Brian as a person amounts to very little. Enumerating in my own mind all that I knew about him, I arrived at the following list:

He is an expatriate American from Madison, Wisconsin, who has lived in Dublin since 2000.

He does indeed live in Rathmines, as can be determined by the postmarks on his letters, and resides only a short distance from Le Fanu's final resting place in Mount Jerome Cemetery.

He is always willing, nay *eager*, to act as my remote research assistant by looking into records available only in Dublin and Belfast archives, which I need for my own Le Fanu research.

He is a devoted enthusiast of the strange tale, that venerable and still lively mode of storytelling with the specific goal of invoking a primal awe in the reader; what M. R. James called 'a pleasing terror'.

He is keen on the lost byways of history and has a knack for sniffing out mysteries within even the driest of documents, then doggedly following lead after lead until he has discovered as many pieces of the hitherto-forgotten puzzle as still remain available to modern eyes.

This knowledge amounts to very little; therefore you can imagine my bewilderment when he began to send me, quite unexpectedly, the stories that are now included in this book.

Brian's fascination with the strange histories he has uncovered in his chosen home have proved infectious, and the joy I felt while first reading them, in the raw, has been redoubled now that he has correlated these tales into a single volume, so that a wider understanding and appreciation for Rathmines has emerged. Not that this joy has been an entirely comfortable one; as you will discover within these pages, the history of Rathmines hides more than a few disturbing patterns which bode ill for those of a careless or over-inquisitive temperament. Brian's own persistence and curiosity have more than once landed him in trouble with local eccentrics, belligerent alcoholics, landlords harbouring a rather brutal intolerance towards trespassers, and led to random encounters with a person or persons perhaps just as dangerous whose motivations remain, as yet, unclear.

When Brian first started sending me these stories, he provided no preface or explanation, inviting no input beyond the occasional question regarding syntax and orthographical errors. It was as if reading these strange stories of local supernatural disturbances allowed me to eavesdrop on ghostly radio transmissions from across the Atlantic. Separated though I may have been by many thousands of miles, I was still somehow drawn into them and made complicit in their telling. But what was their underlying meaning? Had Brian been sending them to me in lieu of the private thoughts he guarded so carefully?

Perhaps someone reading this book can determine the answers to another series of questions that has plagued me ever since these cryptic narratives began to appear: How much in them is truth and how much fiction? Where precisely does Brian's carefully documented research end and the outgrowths of his imagination begin? And are we to accept the narrator's voice and opinions as those of the author, or do they represent a persona? I tried asking Brian these questions after reading each successive story, but he always found a way to routinely, if politely, avoid answering any of them. Not that he has not occasionally let drop a tantalising hint.

There is a curious episode in 'Quis Separabit' in which the narrator mentions purchasing a first edition of Le Fanu's *The House by the Churchyard* in a flea market for the price of six pounds. Those of you who are familiar with the value of such a book are no doubt gasping, and you can well imagine that I did the same. However, Brian's response to my queries was in this case rather more than I expected. I received no immediate response to my email asking him if he had really encountered this edition at such an astoundingly low price. But what I did not foresee, and what continues to amaze me, was my receipt eight days later of a bulky parcel wrapped in brown paper bearing the postmark of Rathmines and containing a remarkably fine copy of *The House by the Churchyard* – all three volumes, printed in London by Tinsley Brothers in 1863. Scrawled lightly in pencil on the inside cover of each volume was '£2'. Between the copyright and title page was a scrap of paper with a brief note in Brian's handwriting:

I hope this helps you with your research. Please take your time with it and return it at your leisure.

Yours sincerely,

Brian

I would have been afraid even to entrust such a treasure to the mail, but that is at least one of many mysteries associated with these tales which we can safely put to rest.

A subject about which there should be no doubt is the existence and location of all the sites mentioned within these stories. Any good map of the city will show each of the sites Brian describes, as will a deft hand and a degree of diligence with an internet search engine.

Considering the passion with which Brian pursues these strange 'stories' of his, I would have expected to hear that he had approached a publisher and was well on the way to seeing at least the first of several specimens in print, but when I brought this up some months ago, he responded as though the thought had never entered his mind. A few months later I was expecting to discover that he had acted upon my suggestion, but he informed me that he had still not contacted anyone. Although he was hesitant at first, he ultimately had no objections to my submitting them on his behalf. This was not the easiest thing to do: I was separated from Brian by an ocean and half a continent, and had to talk around his diffidence and my own inexperience with publishers without making us both sound like lost causes. After the usual round of publishers who may very well have thought just that, I found a sympathetic ear, and the book that resulted from our negotiations rests in your hands.

In the meantime, Brian has continued to send me more ghost stories of Rathmines, the most recent of which concerns St Mary's College and the eccentric ornithologist Ellis Grimwood. There should be enough new stories to fill a second volume some time in the near future. Whether he will take a more active role in submitting this second crop of tales to a publisher is anyone's guess.

Let us all hope that if Mr Showers, in the course of his researches and perambulations, within either the physical world we all share or the world of his private imagination, ever finds himself amidst shades of dubious mortality, they pay less heed, and take less offence to his scrutiny than have their mortal counterparts. And if a friend ever invites you to visit the former Blackberry Fair after dark, find an excuse, any excuse, to decline.

J. R.

I. The Road to Rathmines

Most people do not realise as they go south along South Great George's Street from Dublin's city centre that they are walking a very old path. It is one of the four roads to Dublin, a highway of pre-Norman origin that still feeds the city like a great tributary. This particular road connects Dublin with the not far-distant neighbourhood of Rathmines. At one time Rathmines was a desolate morass of scrub and gorse, of swampy ground and wandering, unbounded rivulets. But from this unwelcoming terrain sprouted first a rural village, then, from tillage land, a booming township, and now a fully urbanised neighbourhood of the ever-expanding city. And Rathmines, built upon the mulch and layered sediment of history, is our destination this evening.

If we follow the old highway away from the city centre the road changes its identity several times – South Great George's Street bypasses onto modern Aungier Street which gives way to Wexford Street and so on

– until we come to Camden Street, and a well-known and oddly named pub called the Bleeding Horse where, like countless travellers before us, we can stop for a nip of your favourite and a short rest. Now, does everyone have a pint? I hope you will indulge me in this opportunity to tell you the evening's first tale. It's called:

The Bleeding Horse

The Bleeding Horse is a local pub, and from its many rooms, balconies and cosy corners you can see how this 'alehouse' has always been popular with both local gossips and the not infrequent solitary tippler, stout in one hand, whiskey in the other. Literary tourists may already be familiar with this pub, as it is not only mentioned briefly in James Joyce's *Ulysses*[1] but also features in Joseph Sheridan Le Fanu's 1845 novel *The Cock and the Anchor*.[2] And ordinary tourists in search of the 'authentic Irish experience' may be familiar with the pub from a favourite local joke: Disoriented tourist asks, 'Do y'all know where the

---

[1] 'I saw him a few times in the Bleeding Horse in Camden street with Boylan, the billsticker.'

[2] 'There stood at the southern extremity of the city, near the point at which Camden Street now terminates, a small, old-fashioned building, something between an alehouse and an inn.'

Bleeding Horse is at?' To which the reply is, 'Why, in the bleedin' barn, I reckon!'

One night while here at the Bleeding Horse I was treated to a story concerning the origin of this pub's unusual name. Admittedly I heard the story from one of the Horse's own arch patrons, and I will not deny that the entire evening was jubilantly riotous and filled with stories of varying veracities, but I will tell you the tale as it was told to me. Though you may, as I did, wish to take it with at least a spoonful of salt.

Some of you may have noticed a painted sign affixed to the front of the building as we entered. For those who are not so observant, it depicts a giant, ash-grey horse's head with tiny droplets of blood trickling from a thin wound in its neck, though this last detail has almost completely faded from the weatherworn sign. Below the disembodied equine is written '1649'. This obviously makes the Bleeding Horse one of Dublin's more venerable drinking establishments, but also – ah, I see a thoughtful eyebrow rise on the more historically minded of you. Of course I will forgive the others for not being at all familiar with the Battle of Rathmines, which occurred on 2 August 1649, the same year that the Bleeding Horse was founded. Admittedly the battle was a minor skirmish as far as these things go. It was something of a coda to the then recently concluded Second English Civil War and a precursor to Oliver Cromwell's subsequent and somewhat destructive invasion of Ireland. Here is what happened:

James Butler, the first Duke of Ormonde and deposed Lord Lieutenant of Dublin, was encamped with his Royalist supporters in the area that is now Rathmines.[3] On the previous day Ormonde had taken the strategically positioned Baggotrath Castle near present-day Baggot Street. On the morning of the second, Ormonde was poised to reclaim the Parliamentarian-held city; though, by all accounts, he was an ineffectual military man. The Earl of Stafford once described Ormonde's demeanour as being that of 'a very staid head', and although Ormonde's army numbered around 11,000 that day, he was still no match for his opponent, the newly installed Governor of Dublin, Colonel Michael Jones and his 4,000 troops.

Had Ormonde attacked immediately, the chances are he would have overtaken Jones' men and restored Dublin to the monarchy. However, after taking Baggotrath Castle, Ormonde inexplicably relaxed his offensive. He decided to bide his time and attack at leisure. His disordered and undisciplined army, composed partly of recently allied Irish Confederate Catholics, had improperly fortified the *ráth*; and in the midst

---

[3] A painting of the Duke of Ormonde by the Studio of Peter Lely, 1660s (NGI 136), is on public display in the National Gallery of Ireland in the Shaw Room of the Dargan Wing.

of this, as detailed in a letter to Charles II, Ormonde decided to take a nap to restore his strength.[4]

Colonel Jones saw this opportunity and managed to rally a cavalry of 1,200 horses in addition to his 4,000 foot soldiers for an immediate attack. Ormonde awoke in a panic to the sound of cannons and gunfire. He was expecting the arrival of Major-General Purcell and 1,500 reinforcements; however, their arrival was long since overdue. Unbeknownst to Ormonde, Purcell had been led astray in the maze of local *bohreens* the evening before by a treacherous guide, and was still a day's journey away.[5] The Parliamentarians launched their attack from a nearby garrison, reclaimed Baggotrath Castle, and then swept around the Royalists' front line in Rathmines to attack from the rear. The Royalists and the Parliamentarians clashed, and for two hours the Battle of Rathmines raged.

Ill-prepared and worried by an erroneous report that Cromwell's army had landed at Ringsend, Ormonde's men broke rank and retreated south towards the Dublin Mountains with Jones in close pursuit. Jones' cavalry caught up with Ormonde's men near the present-day intersection of Palmerston and Cowper Roads. A horrific

---

[4] '*Ráth*' is a small, defensive castle of Norman origin. These ráths at one time were numerous along the outskirts of Dublin, and traces of them can still be seen in modern place names including Rathgar, Rathfarnham, Rathdown, Rathcoole, etc.

[5] '*Bohreen*' is a narrow, rural footpath.

massacre resulted. This absolute defeat both solidified the Parliamentarian victory and insured, at least for the moment, against further Royalist uprisings. As for Ormonde's men: they were buried in mass graves where they fell. And even though the area has been built up over the intervening years, it is still known today as the 'Bloody Fields'; the Royalist army still, presumably, buried lifeless beneath the earth.[6]

By now you are probably wondering how the Bleeding Horse fits in with this history lesson. Well, it all has to do with one Sir William Vaughan, a cavalry commander who fought on the side of the Duke of Ormonde. He was an intimidating and loud man with a red face and a bushy white moustache. His heavy leather boots, fitted with thick soles so that he appeared taller than he actually was, made him an intimidating opponent in any venue, parliament notwithstanding. Sir William's ferocious reputation extended to the battlefield and, true to character, he had put many Roundheads to the sword during the Battle of Rathmines. Augmenting the myth of Sir William was his pure-bred, ash-grey charger, Bucephalus, which he always rode hard into battle with a roaring, Viking-like cry. Sir William and

---

[6] Some historians believe the name 'Bloody Fields' is even older than the Battle of Rathmines. The area is reputed to be the site of a Bristolian settlement that was slaughtered by the local Gaelic clans in 1209. As with the Royalist soldiers, their remains were also supposedly buried *in situ*.

Bucephalus together were an unstoppable war machine – until that day in August. At some point late in the skirmish, Bucephalus purportedly panicked. History does not record what spooked the horse, but we do know that Sir William was thrown from his mount and, in a manner fitting of his own brutality, he was decapitated by one of Colonel Jones' men.[7]

Hours after Sir William's death on the battlefield in Rathmines, an enormous grey warhorse, wounded and bloodied from combat, wandered to the crossroads about half a mile north of the fighting, and into the main room of what was then known as the Falcon Inn. The astonished patrons watched the delirious beast stagger about the room knocking over chairs and tables and upsetting beer mugs. No one dared approach the injured animal for fear that it would topple and crush them beneath its mighty weight. But the patrons hardly had time to react before the beast emitted a final snort and collapsed into a bloody pool upon the floor. Later reports, including a brief account in *Curiosities and Wonderments of the City of Dublin and its Environs* (1736) by Stephen Venables Esq., assert that this bloody stain, despite all efforts, remained where the horse had fallen for decades to follow.

---

[7] It is said that the great Irish Republican martyr, Robert Emmet (1778–1803), kept Vaughan's skull on his writing desk when he was an exile in France. How he came to have the skull and what happened to it when Emmet lost his own head remains a mystery.

Now the landlord of the Falcon was known to support the Parliamentarians, and so naturally he assumed this horse was none other than the legendary Bucephalus. This may very well have been a reasonable assumption, but whether or not the horse in question actually was Bucephalus is a historical detail that has never been verified. Also unverified are the ingredients of the Bleeding Horse's popular dish, 'Sir William's Stew'. From shortly after the Battle of Rathmines until the early twentieth century, the famous stew was served from 'Vaughan's Pot', a large kettle, perpetually heated, to which new ingredients were added daily to the old for over two centuries.

Of course as with all pub gossip it did not take long for the story of Sir William's horse to spread from patron to patron, and from that moment on, the Falcon Inn was, and still is, known as the Bleeding Horse.

'And that's just the half of it,' added Jimmy Corkhill, who was behind the bar on that night when I first heard the story. Everyone's attention locked on Jimmy as he picked up the threads of the tale: 'One night, not long after I started here, I was upstairs wiping down some tables and collecting up the last of the empties. Everyone else went home, but I stayed behind to do a bit more washing up, you see.'

'That's a good lad!' bellowed a red-nosed and scholarly-looking regular named Mr Egan. But the comment was only a pebble; Jimmy still had the floor and the ripple of chuckles subsided in seconds.

'So I was wiping off this one table up there, and I heard something downstairs. A kind of banging, heavy like footsteps. First I thought maybe I forgot to lock the door, you see, so I yelled downstairs: "Sorry, buddy, we're closed!" But whoever it was kept on walking around down there. So I went downstairs and on my way I repeated, more forceful like: "Hey buddy, we're closed! Come back in the morning!" But when I got down to the front room, there was no one there. I checked the side room, but it was empty. And the front door was all locked up tight.'

At this point in the tale some wit from the other side of the pub roared in a thick, north Dublin accent, 'Where's my horse? *Where's my horse!*' and then emitted a long wailing moan meant to approximate a ghost, but only sounded drunken.

The whole pub erupted with laughter, a few people commented 'nice one' to Jimmy, more drinks were poured and the night continued with a fresh story.

Now I may take ghost stories a bit more seriously than most, and I think Jimmy sensed this because later in the evening, when everyone's pint was topped up, he leaned over the counter and whispered in my ear: 'It's all true you know. I told the owner Mr McClean about it the next day. I thought he'd fire me, you see, but he only nodded all grim faced. Said he'd heard it once too, and then he tells me this story.

'One night, a few years ago, he was working here all alone, and he heard footsteps, same as I did, but he described them more like clomping, like a horse's iron shoes on the floorboards. It sounds mad, and if I hadn't heard it myself I wouldn't've believed him either. Then he says to me he heard a loud crash and pint glasses smashing on the floor. When he got downstairs he searched the rooms, checked the front door like I had done, but couldn't find no one. But the owner, he knew something must've been in the pub because a bunch of tables had been tipped over and there was broken glass all over the place.

'Mr McClean was trying to puzzle out what'd happened when out of nowhere something massive bowled him clean over; knocked the wind right out of him. At first he thought maybe he was having a heart attack or a seizure or something. He couldn't move his arms nor legs, so he tells me, and his chest was pressed down so hard that he thought his ribs might splinter and snap. He was pinned under something warm, something invisible – something alive, and it was breathing heavy and strained. Whatever it was, the weight was such that Mr McClean couldn't take even a nip of air to save his own life. He says he must have blacked out, because he didn't wake until the next morning. He was still on the floor where he had fallen the night before.'

Jimmy started to pull another pint for Mr Egan, who had signalled from the far corner.

'Worst of all was the dark stain on the floor.' The barman pointed to a bare and slightly scuffed spot near the corner of the pub by the front door. 'When Mr McClean came to, he was lying in the centre of a large ruddy stain. It hadn't been there before. It wasn't wet either – whatever it was had already dried deep into the floorboards, as if it'd been there for years. Mr McClean said he scrubbed it every night for a week, but scrubbing didn't do nothing. It was nearly a full year before it faded and went away on its own. Some of the people here tonight'd remember it; Mr Egan would for sure.'

'What should I remember, Jimmy?' enquired Mr Egan who had come to fetch his one drink too many.

'That the prices went up last week,' said Jimmy, smiling and giving me a conspiratorial wink.

'Well then, maybe I should just have the university pay my wages directly into your bank account then, eh?' remarked Mr Egan as he took his pint from the bar and slurped off the excess foam. 'Now don't go serving our guest too many tall tales, Jimmy.'

When Mr Egan was out of earshot, Jimmy leaned across the bar and said: 'They laugh about it now, but I know they wouldn't laugh to see that stain again. Not even Mr Egan.' Jimmy paused and then added solemnly, 'It's all true, you know. You couldn't ever pay me enough to stay here alone tonight.'

You will notice as we leave the convivial atmosphere of the Bleeding Horse that the venerable structure is situated at an angle incongruent with the present T-shaped intersection formed by Camden Street and Charlotte Way. The Celtic Tiger scratched the layout of the original crossroads from the map when a large hotel the size of half a city block was erected just behind the pub in 1999. If you look at any recent Ordnance Survey map you will see how the vanished Charlotte Street would have extended from the intersection, through the Bleeding Horse's beer garden, until it connected with the still extant Charlemont Street to the south-east. This was the original highway to Ranelagh, Rathmines' more village-like neighbour to the east.

The other road to disappear beneath the footprint of the hotel was the old Milltown path, which defined the Bleeding Horse's western wall and would have connected with Mount Pleasant Road just on the other side of the Grand Canal.

The third path from the old crossroads, the road to Rathmines, is the only one to survive to the present day. It is still heavily used by commuters who live in the southern neighbourhoods, and it will also be our path as we continue our stroll. Another five southbound minutes brings us to one of the city centre's most southerly neighbourhoods: tiny Portobello, and the evening's next story:

Oil on Canvas

The almost incidental neighbourhood of Portobello owes much of its existence to the Grand Canal, which forms its southern border, and to Portobello Harbour, which was lamentably filled in during the late 1940s. Beside the old harbour, overlooking the Grand Canal, is the former hub of the area: Portobello House, formerly a hotel, which was built by the Grand Canal Company in 1805. The hotel opened on 13 July 1807 and served travellers along the waterways between Dublin and Shannon. In his *Guide Book of Dublin* (1821), John James MacGregor wrote:

> The Grand Canal Hotel, Portobello, is a very fine edifice, situated on the banks of the Grand Canal opposite the pleasant village of Rathmines. It has in front a very handsome portico, and the interior is fitted up with great elegance for the accommodation of families and single gentlemen. The beauty and salubrity of the situation, enlivened by the daily arrival and departure of the canal boats render it a truly delightful residence.'

The black-faced clock that you see today, however, with its distinctive gold numerals and bells housed in the small, roof-top cupola, was not installed until 1914.

The Grand Canal Hotel ceased functioning in 1852 in the wake of the Great Hunger. Shortly thereafter the building became an asylum for 'industrious blind women' run by the Sisters of Charity, and from 1898 until 1971 Portobello House served as a private nursing home for the aged. It was in this nursing home that painter Jack B. Yeats, younger brother of Ireland's famous poet and statesman, spent his final years. Yeats stopped painting professionally in 1955; and in the months leading up to his death, he was unable to paint at all, much to his increasing frustration. This was primarily due to a decline in eyesight, an affliction he shared with his elder brother. Yeats died on 28 March 1957 and was interred in Mount Jerome Cemetery in nearby Harold's Cross.

In the years following the passing of the celebrated painter, the nursing home's employees, with an alarming frequency, found 'stains of complementary and contrasting hues daubed upon the walls': the nurses reported 'all shades of white, shadowy blues, lush yellows, dark greens, and poppy field reds'. The damage was often discovered in rooms known to have been locked, or on sections of wall that no one could have got at without having been caught out. Of course, the staff and residents invariably denied all responsibility.

The 'artistic disturbances' became such a problem that Dr Bellowes, the nursing home's exasperated administrator, in a move that drew much public criticism, called on psychical investigator Colonel Roger W. Ogilvie-Forbes.[8] Ogilvie-Forbes was at that time lodging in Rathmines while investigating the 'Beast of Belgrave Square' attacks. In addition to his many other proficiencies, Ogilvie-Forbes was a knowledgeable art enthusiast. During his investigation of Portobello House he noted that the texture and composition of the wall markings, though mostly indefinite shapes, were, 'exceptionally similar to Yeats' distinctive expressionist style', and that they were made with 'nothing more mysterious than what appears to be oil paint'. Ogilvie-Forbes was unable to offer a suitable explanation, though subsequent tests confirmed that the substance was indeed oil paint of the Windsor & Newton variety, available from any art supply shop.

For many years it was not uncommon for the elderly and even-tempered cleaning lady, Mrs Barry, to report loud stomping and banging noises during her pre-dawn rounds of the building. They always emanated from 'near Mr Yeats' old room', she said, and had a manner of 'spoilt frustration about them'. The stomping occurred with such

---

[8] Colonel Roger W. Ogilvie-Forbes served as the president of the York Society for Psychical Research in England from 1962–1992.

frequency that the unflappable Mrs Barry soon came to ignore it as she went about her daily chores. Perhaps this is why it came as a surprise when a nurse found her one morning seated on the floor in a dim recess of the upper hallway. She held one hand to her head as if in a swoon; the other was clutching a crucifix she wore around her neck on a thin gold chain. A hasty retirement followed, and until her dying day, Mrs Barry refused to speak of what had happened to her that morning in the upper hall.

The supernormal activity ceased altogether during a 1987 renovation when a previously unknown Yeats painting was discovered in a disused attic cupboard. The untitled and undated painting shows a weary, pale grey horse galloping across a shallow stream surrounded by meadows in a prismatic scintillation of moonlight. By all accounts the painting, posthumously referred to as *Horse in Moonlight*, is a masterpiece. Those who have seen it compare it to Yeats' famous oil painting *For the Road* (1951), although most feel *Horse in Moonlight*'s powerful atmosphere and haunting melancholy far surpass the better-known work.[9]

There are two further facts in this case that, while extraordinary, are generally disregarded by the serious and sober-minded. The first is that the painting is not

---

[9] *For the Road*, arguably Yeats' most celebrated painting, is on permanent display in the National Gallery.

entirely unfamiliar to Yeats scholars at all. Among Yeats' unpublished personal papers in the Yeats Archive at the National Gallery is a sketchbook filled with preliminary pencil sketches for *Horse in Moonlight*. While the finished painting has no date, the sketches certainly do. There are twelve in total: the earliest is dated 17 December 1956; the last is dated 27 March 1957 – one day before Yeats' death. The second fact is even more peculiar. The worker who found the painting made an unusual comment about his discovery in an interview with the *Irish Independent*: 'I accidentally smudged the corner of it with my thumb. I don't think the paint was entirely dried when I picked it up.'

The painting is now part of the National Gallery of Ireland's Yeats collection and is listed in their catalogue as: '*Horse in Moonlight*, unknown date. Purchased from the Portobello College of Business (1987). Oil on canvas, 35 x 45 cm, NGI 24027–7.' To my knowledge the painting has never been put on public display.

Portobello House's current incarnation is that of a business college, and since the institute opened in 1988, immediately following the aforementioned renovation, there have been no further reports of 'artistic disturbances' much to the delight, I am sure, of the school's board of directors. And despite two centuries of history, Portobello House still stoically overlooks the canal and beyond its southern banks to Rathmines.

Favourite No. 7 Omnibus

An oil painting by the English artist David Snagg shows Portobello House as it stood in the halcyon days of 1809, two years after it opened as a hotel. It depicts gentlemen with walking sticks and ladies with parasols strolling on the lawn near the lock; a canal-boat approaches in the distance. This splendid painting now hangs on the first floor of the period Georgian museum at 29 Fitzwilliam Street and is available for public viewing without prior appointment. If you should see this painting first hand, you will notice that the horizon line bends, rather unusually, to give the viewer an impossible stereoscopic perspective that does not in actuality exist. Jutting into view at the far left side of Snagg's canvas is a bridge spanning the water at the Grand Canal's sixth lock. This bridge is known locally as the Portobello Bridge; but local tradition, in this case, is not exactly accurate. The bridge's real

name is revealed on two overlooked plaques affixed to its north-west and south-east sides. They read: 'La Touche Bridge, 1791'.[10]

La Touche Bridge was named after David Digges La Touche de Rompiers, a French Huguenot who served alongside William III of Orange in the Battle of the Boyne in 1690. After the battle, and a short time in the crinoline trade, La Touche established a powerful, eponymous bank just across the road from Newcomen & Co. on Castle Street.[11] The La Touche family soon became a dynasty of sorts that would affect Dublin's economic and political climate for generations. If truth be told, David La Touche Esq., Digges La Touche's grandson, was in fact the treasurer of the Grand Canal Company at the time of the bridge's dedication.

La Touche Bridge and the roads leading up to it on either side have now been redesigned into a gentle gradient beginning well before the bridge itself. Aside from periodic motor crashes, this gradual slope is of no particular note to the modern driver other than the not-insignificant vista it provides of Rathmines and, on sunny days, a rather eye-catching view of the Dublin Mountains pressed against the sky beyond. But

---

[10] The current plaques are not the bridge's first. The original nameplate was recovered from the James Street Basin and is now on display in Dublin's Civic Museum on William Street South.

[11] Thus, an old Dublin joke goes: 'Why is Castle-street like a river? Answer: Because it runs between two banks.'

in the mid nineteenth century La Touche Bridge was far steeper. It was a dangerous gauntlet for drivers of the old horse-drawn omnibuses, which, unlike today's buses, were run to stringent timetables.

Over the centuries the Rathmines stretch of the Grand Canal, which La Touche Bridge spans, has seen its fair share of calamities. Some say that this particular expanse of waterway is even prone to them. Since the canal opened in 1756 there have been: numerous suicides; countless drownings, one as recent as 2003; the capsizing in 1792 of a passage boat with one hundred and fifty travellers bound for County Kildare; and perhaps the single most tragic and memorable misfortune of all – an accident in 1861 involving the ill-fated Favourite No. 7 Omnibus and its six unfortunate passengers.

At about 9.20 p.m., on Saturday 6 April 1861, the Favourite No. 7 Omnibus was heading north along Rathmines Road. The 'bus departed from Rathgar and was due to terminate at Nelson's Pillar on Sackville Street.[12] It was pulled by two large draught horses and carried eight passengers. It stopped at the top of the bridge and let two disembark. Six remained on board when the conductor, a chap by the name of Patrick Costello, signalled the all clear to the driver. Heavy rain in

---

[12] Sackville Street may be more familiar today as O'Connell Street, which has been its name since 1924. The Nelson Pillar was destroyed by an IRA bomb on 8 March 1966, and was recently replaced with the Millennium Spire.

Dublin is common in the springtime, and this night was no different. The steep bridge was slick with water and visibility was at a minimum. Badger, a stout grey horse, and his companion, a bay mare, had reliably pulled the No. 7 for years, but on this night something spooked the latter of the two equines, causing the harness to catch in the pole-chain. Patrick Costello disembarked to calm the horses, but did not appear to be concerned with any impending danger. According to a report in *The Freeman's Journal* on the following Monday:

> [The horses] both got restive and began to back in the direction of Rathmines. [The driver, Patrick Hardy,] turned their heads towards the east with the intention of making them go up the incline of the hill at an angle. This involved the partial locking of the four wheels … The back part of the bus came in contact with the wooden fence between the Lock and the road. The back wheels went over the granite kerb. The horses pulled, but in vain.

A witness stated at the inquest that the bridge's wooden fence, undoubtedly rotted from years of dirty weather, 'yielded like straw' and the omnibus, horses and all, plunged backwards into the lock chamber. The noise of the 'bus splintering against the granite sides of the lock and the terrified snorting of the horses as they fell must have been horrible. From the passengers, however, not a sound was emitted, whether because terror had deprived them of utterance, or the shock of the fall had stunned them. The horses fell between the omnibus and the bridge where they struggled for their lives, and for some time after the fall they kicked their hoofs against the wooden breakwater. The 'bus came to a rest at the bottom of the lock, its door, the only means of escape, facing downwards.

You can see today that the lock is quite deep, twenty-four feet to be exact, and on the evening in question it was already half-filled with water. In the panic and confusion of the moment, O'Neill, the lock-keeper, opened the upper sluice. 'In the name of God, O'Neill, what have you done?' one onlooker cried out.

'I'll float the 'bus,' was O'Neill's reply.

It would be an understatement to say that the result was not quite what he had hoped – the lock flooded with water, submerging all but the upended front of the 'bus. As soon as the mistake was realised, the lock-keeper scrambled to drain the chamber, but by then it was already too late.

By this time a small crowd of onlookers had assembled to watch what was already a considerable tragedy, though with the lock still draining, there was admittedly little anyone could do. Police Constable Gaffney was the first on the scene. He promptly rescued from the lock the driver, Patrick Hardy, who had miraculously leapt clear of the falling horses and escaped with only a broken arm.

The Freeman's Journal continues: 'When the water

was let off from the lock, so as to expose the top of the Bus, P.C. Gaffney and Private Smith of the 4th Light Dragoons [who arrived shortly after Gaffney] got a cleaver and hatchets and with the aid of a ladder got on to the roof of the Bus, broke a hole in the roof and took out the [six] bodies.' The first to be fished from the shattered wreck was Mrs O'Connell, scarcely alive and still clutching her infant in her arms. The baby, however, was dead. Private Smith worked to revive Mrs O'Connell, but without success. Before she was 'hurried off into eternity' she was heard to mutter to Smith: 'Where's our driver?'

Also among the deceased were Michael Gunn, father of brothers John and Michael Gunn, who later founded the Gaiety Theatre on King Street in 1871; and the noted painter Horace W. Leech. Leech was famous for his portraits of prominent members of the Protestant ascendancy, including the famous solicitor George Bennett Q.C., Lieutenant-Colonel James Balcombe and Sir William Wilde. As each successive victim was retrieved from the wreck and laid out on the bridge, one onlooker remarked: 'The appearance of the bodies presented a most touching sight. All looked calm and placid, as if no struggle supervened in the calamitous moment.'

The newspaper reports were damning, particularly those in *The Irish Times*: 'Was the driver a steady and careful man? Where was the conductor? [H]e escaped, and there is no reason why he should not have helped the passengers to escape also. There are a thousand rumours afloat, and they who could give decisive testimony are all dead.'

The verdict given by the jury at the inquest was that 'every one exerted himself to the best of his judgment' and no blame was ascribed to any party. On the coroner's report was written: *Incussus in uno, incussus in omnibus*, which is then further clarified in English as, 'a fatal bodily shock to the omnibus' occupants as caused by the vehicle falling into the Lock by accident due to adverse weather conditions'.[13] This, then, was determined the official cause of death, not drowning. And though everyone, including the lock-keeper, was exonerated of responsibility, those involved seemed weighed down by what we would today call survivor's guilt.

The first to die was O'Neill, the lock-keeper, who took his own life one Sunday the following year when he 'bound his ankles and legs up tight with sturdy twine and threw himself bodily into the very same lock he managed for thirty-five years'. The *Evening Chronicle* was the only newspaper to report the brief and uninteresting facts. These facts concern prolonged melancholy and moroseness, and I will not bore you with them here. Anyone with an interest in this sort of thing can read more in the *Chronicle's* 'Dublin Notes' department.[14]

---

[13] 'Struck by one, struck by all.' It would appear that the coroner in charge of the inquest, Dr Roger Johnson, had a playful sense of gallows humour, especially given the apparent pun on the word 'omnibus'.

[14] 'Lock-keeper in Tragic Canal Suicide', *Evening Chronicle*. Monday 7 April 1862, p. 4.

The second to die was Patrick Costello, the conductor. By all accounts, Costello was never the same in the wake of the accident and ceased his employment with the omnibus company shortly thereafter. He became something of a recluse and that summer took up residency in the shelter of a large tree in the middle of a quiet paddock near Rathgar. The farmer tolerated him for a couple of months before complaining to the town commissioners, who promptly acted. Destitute and having no immediate family to support him, Costello became a ward of the state. For the next five years he was confined to the Richmond District Lunatics Asylum on Brunswick Street, then situated at the edge of the city. Upon his release on the first weekend of April 1866, Costello was reportedly heading west along Brunswick Street towards the countryside when he was struck dead under the wheels of a large black omnibus of unknown provenance. The only witness to the accident was the driver of a Guinness delivery wagon, who was also forced off the road by the speeding 'bus. 'It set the heart across me,' said the drayman. 'She [the omnibus] came out of nowhere. The poor man, he was all hunched over with his back to the road like he knew something was coming. But he didn't see it until it was too late. I still remember that horrible look in his eye as he died there on the road, the poor man.'[15]

---

[15] 'Highway Death leaves Metropolitan Police Mystified', *The Irish Times*. 9 April 1866, p. 2.

For a while the Metropolitan Police sought information leading to the apprehension of the black omnibus' driver, but with no known family to exert continued pressure on the police, the case was eventually dropped. No one was ever identified in connection with the accident.

The last to die was Patrick Hardy, the driver of the Favourite No. 7 Omnibus. Unlike the others, his death was more prolonged and painful due to tormented memories intensified by the effects of alcohol abuse, to which he wholly succumbed after the accident. Hardy lived in a small thatched cottage with his ever-tolerant wife in an area next to a bend in the Swan River known as 'The Chains', near modern-day Wynnefield Road. Although pardoned of any responsibility, Hardy quit his job as an omnibus driver immediately following the inquest and took up residency at Burke's public house, not more than a few yards away from his front door.[16]

Until his death in 1892, Hardy never strayed far from the well-worn path between his cottage and the pub. And he was never seen to cross a street for the rest of his life. As he shuffled to the drinking establishment every afternoon, he always kept one eye on the road. When sober, which was not often, he displayed an edgy disposition, not to be mistaken for impoliteness, whether peering ex-

---

[16] Burke's Pub is today known as Martin B. Slattery's. In the late nineteenth century Anthony O'Grady, who later opened the Stella Picture Theatre in 1923, purchased the pub and for a time it was also known as O'Grady's.

pectantly into the distance during conversation, or glanc-
ing over his perpetually hunched shoulders. But if given
enough to drink he always became more genial, and
since he was in a state of constant drunkenness, he was a
generally well-liked character. For the price of a few pints,
and if he had not yet passed out, he would treat random
strangers to a version of events on the night of 6 April 1861.
In 1891 that stranger was Dr R. M. Huberty of Manchester, who interviewed Hardy and recorded the anecdote for
his book, *An Examination of Imbibed Alcohols*: [17]

We turn now to Ireland, whose working class is known to
be plagued by a largely uncontrolled compulsion to drink.
Mr Patrick Hardy of Rathmines is a most singular and
persistent case of alcohol-induced delusions. Our meeting
lasted for one hour, and in that time he drank four pints
of that locally produced noxious black brew to which he is
horribly addicted. His short stature and timorous nature
are as such that one cannot help but to be reminded of a
frightened hedgehog. His wrinkled features are beyond his
years, and his hair and nails are both long and unkempt.
Despite this state of dishevelment, the proprietor of the
establishment knew his name and poured his drink before
we even sat down, a testament to the social acceptability of
the ethylated condition.

Mr Hardy's severe condition stems from a tragedy he
experienced some thirty years ago. By all accounts he was a
normal and healthy man before the catastrophe. The event
in question concerns an omnibus that fell into Dublin's

---

[17] Huberty, Dr R. M., *An Examination of Imbibed Alcohols; their Addictive qualities, Harmful natures, and Delusional effects* (Johnson Street Press,
Manchester, 1892), pp. 435–6.

Grand Canal. Mr Hardy was the driver, and the only man to go into the lock and escape with his life. The other five passengers and one infant drowned. Since the accident, Mr Hardy has shifted all feelings of guilt and personal fault to an external source. For these past thirty years he has been under the delusion that a phantasm, what he terms a *monster*, caused the accident. The extent of this belief is thorough and pervades his memory.

Mr Hardy tells the story in his own words: 'Something spooked the horses that night. It was some sort of monster. I know what I seen. You don't believe me, do you? I was doing the number seven route like I always done. Normally I bring the 'bus up on the bridge and it was never a problem, even when the rain's as dense as this here pint. Costello pounded me the all clear on the side of the 'bus, and just as I was about ready to go, Old Badger, he starts panicking. From the crest of the bridge I can see right down Richmond Street. I'll never forget the sight of the monster when I first seen it. It had blinding white eyes it did, low to the ground like two burning lamps, and as it got closer they started flashing brighter at me! I could hear the thing growling as it come closer, and then it starts making these horrible trumpet screams. You don't believe me, do you? I knew it was aiming to smash right into us, so I tried to get the horses to go at an angle, to move us out of the way, like, and give that screaming damned thing a wide berth. Pretty soon the old bay mare starts snorting and pulling at the pole-chain.

There was nothing I could do to stop the pair of them, but Costello got down to try. The horses started backing up, and the 'bus turned at an angle sharp like. Just as I hear the 'bus snapping through the barrier – the monster vanishes right into thin air! I jumped out of me seat just as the 'bus fell into the lock. Somehow them horses never landed on me. They always were good horses. I've never been able to stop thinking about that monster or all them people that went down into the lock. A 'bus needs a driver if it's ever going to get where it's going to. You don't believe me, do you? There was that one young lady, prettiest face I ever seen, they pulled her out alive. She was still clutching her wee one. She knew she was dying. She looked right at me and I could see it in her eyes. O'Connell, that was her name. Pretty young lady, I'll never forget her face. "What about our driver?" she said. "What about our driver?" I'll not forget those words ever. I remember them clear as day. You don't believe me, do you?'

Hardy passed away the same year Dr Huberty's book was published. When Hardy's body was found, he was slumped over the counter in his usual seat at the end of the bar farthest from the main road. The barman thought Hardy was dozing, as he was often prone to do. Being a regular customer he was only rousted from slumber at last call, and it was only then that the barman realised that a corpse had been sitting all night at his bar. Local legend holds that Hardy finished his pint before dying. Although years of heavy drink were certainly a factor, he is said to have died of natural causes. Naturally the wake was held at O'Grady's Pub, as Burke's was by then called, and Hardy was interred in a small plot in Mount Jerome.

Given the profound psychological impact the Favourite No. 7 tragedy had on the community, you may not be surprised to learn that it has since been woven into the fabric of local folklore. In Father Bernie Kilpatrick's landmark work, *Phantoms and Apparitions of South Dublin*, we learn that sightings of a 'black carriage' heading north along Rathmines Road is not uncommon, with the earliest recorded account dating to the mid 1890s.[18] Kilpatrick believes that the black carriage is none other than the revenant of the Favourite No. 7 Omnibus, and he bases this supposition on a number of eyewitness accounts he has collected over the decades.

In 1916 a factory worker on his way home from second shift was almost run down one morning by the black carriage: 'It disappeared right before my eyes when it reached the crest of the bridge,' he recalled. A librarian working late one night in 1920 saw the black carriage from the library window; he described it rather ponderously as 'a nineteenth century-style omnibus silently pulled by two vaporous steeds without legs'. In 1955 a drayman saw the black carriage early one morning as he was going about his deliveries: 'It was the queerest thing I ever seen. The carriage was black with five pale white passengers. And the two horses that were pulling it – I swear their hooves never once touched the ground.' Of all the accounts catalogued in Kilpatrick's book, there is one detail that many have in common: the black carriage is always driverless.

The black carriage's cultural significance seems to echo that of the legendary banshee. Like the banshee, to

---

[18] The Death Coach, or *cóiste bothar* in Irish, is a figure that features in folklore throughout Ireland, Scotland and Britain. It functions as either a portent of death, like the *bean sídhe*, or as a psychopomp that guides souls to the afterlife.

see the black carriage signifies impending death or catastrophe. A quick survey of Slattery's patrons will confirm that this is something today's residents of Rathmines still firmly believe. Indeed, one of the most spectacular encounters with the apparition resulted in a near fatal automobile accident on 6 April 1961.

A young man by the name of Padráig O'Heardy was driving home one night from a friend's house in Clontarf. As he approached La Touche Bridge, heading south on Richmond Street, he lost control of his car. It had been raining that night, and the car skidded across the rain-slicked road towards the bridge, where it smashed through the barrier and went into the lock chamber. Fortunately the lock was nearly empty, and an off-duty fireman who was passing at the time was quick to action. Aside from a mild concussion and a clean break of his left radius and ulna, O'Heardy was unharmed. The excuse for the crash given in the police report was that O'Heardy had too much drink on him. On the surface it is a fairly simple open and shut case. What makes the accident notable is the gossip that developed afterwards – such news travels quickly in Dublin neighbourhoods, and O'Heardy happened to be a local Rathmines man. Kilpatrick later interviewed him for *Phantoms and Apparitions of South Dublin*, and the excerpt is worth reprinting here in its entirety:

It wasn't drink like the *gardaí* said. I'd always heard of the black carriage from me ma and me grandma, but until I seen it, I never believed it. When I did see it, I immediately had this feeling in my gut like something bad was going to happen. The carriage was just standing there at the top of the bridge. It was black. There were horses – two of them, I remember. It almost looked like one of them horse drawn carriages from that Dracula film a few years back. I knew I was going too fast and was going to hit it. I braked hard, but because of all the rain, the car kept skidding towards the bridge. I thought I would smash into the black carriage for sure. I didn't know what to do, so I flashed my high beams, and I started honking the horn so much it would wake the devil. Just as I was about to hit the carriage, it disappeared. I know you don't believe me, but that's what it did. It just disappeared. The next thing I remember was the sound of the barrier breaking and then everything went black. When I woke up I was in St James' all bandaged up. I was real lucky that day. I always had the feeling I shouldn't have survived that accident. Like that black carriage was there waiting for me. I stopped driving after that night. I take the bus now. It's much safer.

On the evening of 6 April 2006, a full 145 years after the tragedy, I made my way to La Touche Bridge and made myself comfortable on one of the well-lit benches that now sit beside the lock. The water between the sluices was calm and deep black. This was the 'yawning chasm' and 'black abyss' described by the reporters, perhaps not even melodramatically. What did I expect to happen in the minutes between 9.20 and 9.30 p.m. when the Favourite No. 7 Omnibus met its fate? Was I waiting for two ethereal horses pulling the black carriage to gallop amidst modern-day traffic? Or for the disembodied din of the omnibus tumbling into the lock? Perhaps I awaited the white and fish-nibbled faces of the dead to stare up at me from the black abyss. But not so much as a ripple broke the surface of the black waters, and the only sounds to be heard were those of double-decker buses rocketing across the bridge, and the water as it cascaded over the lower sluice. The sheet of placid water reflected the old Grand Canal Hotel and divulged none of its secrets. The only thing of note to happen that night was when the lamp perched on the bridge's western railing flickered and died. Instinctively I took my watch from my pocket. It read 9.24 p.m.

II. Rathmines Road Lower

La Touche Bridge provides a splendid vantage point from which to survey the vista of Rathmines Road Lower, one of south Dublin's main arteries. From the bridge's elevated apex you can see many of the neighbourhood's notable features: the mid nineteenth-century terraced houses lining the eastern side of the road like a steep cliff; the verdigris dome of Mary Immaculate, with Our Lady of Refuge perched at the tip of the portico; and the red sandstone town hall with its clock face that on summer nights glows like a low-hanging moon. If weather conditions are right, you will even see the gentle Dublin Mountains in the distance. Save for a few modern blemishes easily removed with an imaginative squint of the eye, this is how Rathmines Road Lower and its skyline have looked for almost one hundred years.

Meones' Beast

In the fourteenth century this entire area was presided over by a fortified castle, or *ráth*, that stood somewhere between Rathmines Road and Cullenswood, a once heavily wooded area that is now part of present-day Ranelagh.[19] The de Meones family came to Dublin from Hampshire, England, with the Archbishop de Derlington in 1279 when the latter was elevated to the archbishopric. In 1326 the great soldier and warrior, Gilbert de Meones, moved into the *ráth*, and consequently controlled most of the surrounding land.

Sir Gilbert was known throughout the land for his strength, courage and righteousness, and over the decades his many exploits developed into legend. One

---

[19] Take care not to confuse the de Meones' *ráth* with the two other structures that have been called 'Rathmines Castle'. Sir George Radcliffe built the first Rathmines Castle in the 1630s near the present site of Palmerston Park. The other Rathmines Castle was built in 1820 by Colonel Wynne and stood near Rathmines Road Upper. Like the old *ráth*, not a trace remains of either castle.

of the most repeated accounts, whether true or untrue, concerns his defeat of a great shaggy monster known as Meones' Beast.[20] The beast is said to have lived near a bend in the Swan River close to the old Rathmines highway. From its evil den it killed livestock and feasted on hapless travellers. In the nineteenth century, Meones' Beast was a popular subject of broadsheets and ballads, including this anonymous example written circa 1840:

'How Sir Gilbert Slew the Suaine River Beast'

Brave Sir Gilbert met the Beast,
That rumbled near the Suaine.
Said the beast with gnashing teeth,
'I'll tear your heart in twain.'

Dark yellow eyes and mane of black,
Its tusks were stained with Blood.
Fair Christian souls it would attack,
Crushing bones into the Mud.

Sir Gilbert called unto his God,
With Spear brandished long and true,
He leapt and met that Darkling Dog,
And drove his Spike straight through.

---

[20] Meones' Beast will remind many of the Lampton Worm legend of north-east England. I am told by an acquaintance that contemporary Irish artist Jonathan Barry was commissioned to paint a series of scenes from the history of Rathmines for permanent display in the local library. The first painting he produced was of Sir Gilbert slaying the infamous beast. However, the head librarian felt the depiction of the beast was so horrific that the entire project was scrapped.

The Suaine didst roil and run with Red,
Above the Clouds abated.
To Meonesráth Hall he brought its Head,
Brave Sir Gilbert thence was feted.

By 1382 Gilbert's scion William had designated himself Lord Meonesráth after his seat of power. Local tongues corrupted and inverted this name over the centuries until it became Ráthmeones and, ultimately, as we know it today, Rathmines. History does not record why or when the de Meones family quit the area, but we do know that their tenancy of the *ráth* was preceded by a man named Richard de Welton. It is easily conceivable that had de Welton been a better monster slayer, we might instead have lived in Rathwelton. The exact location of de Meones' *ráth* was neither remembered by the yeomanry after the land was divided and sold, nor by cartographers who did not memorialise it as 'ruins' on any extant map. But the name given by the illustrious family remains, and today more than 36,000 people call Rathmines their home.

Shortly after crossing La Touche Bridge and proceeding south along Rathmines Road, you will notice a nondescript and ultimately dead-end lane stretching to the west. This is tiny Blackberry Lane, as evidenced by a sign bolted to the adjacent terrace, and in days past it was literally neither here nor there. The east–west lane was once a narrow and much lengthier *bohreen* beaten through the dense foliage between the Earl of Meath's lands to the south and the old Farm of St Sepulchre to the north.

It should arouse no curiosity that neither estate claimed this stretch of ground, as for countless generations it was primarily utilised by the dead. Until 1850, the lane served as a corpse road – a path used not only by funeral processions, but also, according to belief, by souls of the deceased. Prior to 1850, Blackberry Lane terminated in a former Celtic graveyard that once lay just north of where the current church now stands. Like the faerie paths of western Ireland, these betwixt and between roads are only obstructed at the risk of disturbing the entities that dwell in such places. Buildings that are 'in the way' or constructions erected in a 'contrary place' often suffer peculiar problems. And as you may have guessed, one such example is the subject of our next tale.

Quis Separabit

Blackberry Lane meets Rathmines Road at an almost imperceptibly oblique angle, echoing the course of the original corpse road. If you stand in the middle of the lane and angle yourself correctly, you will see that the old path would have continued across Rathmines Road and passed directly through number 44 Fortescue Terrace. The terrace was built in 1850 during a time when families were fleeing the high taxes and urban decay of Dublin's city centre. The first family to live in number 44 reported all manner of disturbances in the house and back garden. It would take ages combing through old newspapers to find all the grievances levelled against the house, but I have heard that the young son of the last family to live there frequently complained of seeing faces in the dark before moving out. After that, the building was run as a lodging house, and no one had to stay there longer than necessary.

Number 44's neoclassical portico and fanlight window are clearly Georgian in style, but the second- and third-storey windows above the door are curiously misaligned and belie the symmetry of which that style is so fond. The decorative latticework that stretches across the lower half of the first-floor windows is reminiscent of the shallow, wrought-iron balconies found in New Orleans' French Quarter. Although quite common in other parts of the city, no other house in this particular terrace duplicates the feature. Another aspect unique to number 44 is the large stable passage that leads through the ground floor to the stable yard behind the house. Number 44 does not have the same mews access provided to the rest of the terrace by Fortescue Lane, and so this passage compensates by providing direct admittance into the stable yard from Rathmines Road.

For generations of Dubliners this stable passage served as the entrance to a Dickensian-like jumble known as the Blackberry Fair. Although the market closed in 2002, anyone who attended even once will retain vivid memories. You were always met at the front gates by a three-legged and overly friendly black dog. He greeted each shopper with a thick, pink tongue and leaned heavily against your leg if you stopped to pet him. The black dog accompanied you from the footpath and through the stable passage, which was invariably lined with broken rocking horses, battered steamer trunks and old pub fittings. When you reached the end of the tunnel, the dog always stopped and, with a whimper, watched you until you disappeared into the rambling labyrinth of makeshift stalls and corrugated tin shacks. Presumably the nameless brute belonged to one of the vendors, and its seemingly innocuous habit of refusing to enter the market is indicative of what lay within. The sensitivities of animals to the supernatural are always much stronger than our own.

If you ever needed to sell your old records, have your fortune told, buy a chipped porcelain statue of St Patrick, a lens-less telescope or used baby clothes, the Blackberry Fair was your destination. Though venerated by patrons and even by a certain set of non-patrons, the fair never shook off its disreputable status as a junk market. Despite this, prizes could be sought here with some hope and, on rare occasion, even found. Once I found a Victorian 'Railway Time Keeper' pocket watch in perfect working order in a bric-a-brac shop in the far corner of the market. The lady who ran the shop had greasy, grey hair and was missing an eye; the empty space had healed over with a patch of thick, fibrous scar tissue. She slurped Lyons tea from a cracked mug while her remaining eye watched me like a sentinel from the moment I entered the shop until the moment I left, prize ticking in hand. She had refused to accept any more than a fiver for the watch – a criminally low price for such an item.

Bibliophiles among you will be envious to learn that, while searching through an old suitcase full of used books, I found an 1863 first edition copy of Le Fanu's *The House by the Churchyard*, all three volumes, somehow overlooked by collectors. A sign taped to the inside of the lid read 'HARDBACKS £2, PAPERBACKS £1'. I went inside and asked the scarf-clad old man to be sure, assuming he would recognise the volume's proper value. But he only seemed upset that I had distracted him from his newspaper. Without a word he pointed to the sign: HARDBACKS £2 each. Six pounds is what I paid for all three volumes; you will get no argument from me. There may be a hint of gloating in my tone, but I hope I have provided you with some proof that curious objects do turn up in the market from time to time. You have to wonder how such bargains find their way to a place like the Blackberry Fair.

But what of the haunting I promised? Personally I prefer fictional ghost stories to 'true' ones. True hauntings tend to leave me feeling unsatisfied and are often narratively mundane: a friend of a friend once encountered an indistinct mist on a staircase; a harmless, if inexplicable, cold spot leaves you reaching for your jumper; or if you are really lucky, something, possibly an irritable poltergeist, hurls a telephone at you. Inevitably these encounters with the unexplained do not develop past statistics and catalogue entries. You may come away

perplexed by the incident, but with no deeper understanding of supernatural mysteries. However, this is not
the case with the Blackberry Fair.

A sign still bolted to the front of number 44 reads:
'OPEN FROM DAWN 'TIL DUSK' – an incidental *caveat* for
the few who do not know that after sundown the Blackberry Fair becomes the exclusive haunt of a particularly
violent apparition. This spectre is locally synonymous
with the bogeyman and regularly invoked by incensed
mothers, who can still be heard to threaten: 'If you think
you're bold, I'll go fetch the Blackberry Man on you.'

It seems that the fair's management, either through
tradition, respect or genuine fear of the infamous Blackberry Man, has always stringently enforced the dawn 'til
dusk rule. A vendor once showed me his lease, which
dated back to 1982. He pointed out a clause which stated:
'All vendors will promptly cease trading before dusk and
will not linger about the premises after twilight. Those
who do so risk immediate eviction.' His father's lease
from the mid 1940s contained the same clause, he said.

At closing time the gates to the stable passage are
shut and padlocked, as are the front gates along the
footpath. Even the local hooligans with their inbred
superstitions know that the back premises are strictly
off limits. Anyone who enters the fair after the sun has
disappeared from the late afternoon sky does so at their
own risk.

The Blackberry Fair shut down for good in February of 2002. Those who were around at that time might remember the incident that prompted its closure. It was reported in all the local newspapers, and even picked up by some international ones. On a cold Saturday morning in late February, the market's proprietor discovered the remains of three Englishmen. The bodies of Rex Liebl, Geoff Kendes and Eric Ensine, all in their mid twenties, were found in the north-east corner of the market, propped up against the bookseller's stall opposite a life-size statue of the Virgin Mary. There had been no sign of struggle, and despite the state of their faces and lack of fingers for fingerprints, their identities were not difficult to confirm. In their wallets were numerous forms of identification, including driving licences, video rental cards and laminated memberships for an internet-based ghost-hunting organisation called The International Cold Spot Society.[21]

For those not familiar with amateur 'ghost-hunting', it has become a popular pastime in recent years, spurred on by a number of US and UK television programmes that purport to 'investigate' alleged hauntings. These decidedly non-scientific shows have but a single purpose: to boost good ratings, with little regard for authenticity. Much to the regret of professional parapsychologists and

---

[21] The website (www.coldspotsociety.org), including its message board, was taken off line in the wake of the tragedy.

psychical researchers, amateur groups emulating these kinds of television programmes have sprouted up all around the world. Messrs Liebl, Kendes and Ensine belonged to one of these groups.

According to the police report, the three ghost-hunters hailed from the Toxteth neighbourhood of Liverpool, and planned their Dublin adventure on the Cold Spot Society message board. Their plan was to gain access to the market after nightfall by scaling the back garden wall from Fortescue Lane.[22] Here the stone wall is not much higher than seven and a half feet. They carried little by way of equipment – torches, digital cameras and note pads – and so the climb over the wall would have been easy. Once over they found themselves amongst the narrow laneways and heavy shadows of the market. Had they not brought torches they would have found themselves in thick darkness, for the market is not well lit. There has never been a need for much lighting. As on every other night, the green dome of the church blotted out the moon in the southern sky, while the houses of Fortescue Terrace acted as a thick curtain between the intrepid ghost-hunters and the relative safety of Rathmines Road.

Events leading up to the Liverpudlians' deaths can be pieced together from the images found in their cameras. Various candid photos show the young trio packing

---

[22] In the 1930s the then proprietor of the market bought the houses numbered 40 and 42, and expanded the market into their back gardens.

their bags in Liverpool, checking into a dingy hostel on Gardiner Street, posing with James Joyce on Talbot Street, and drinking Guinness in Temple Bar, grins extending past the edges of their faces. Only three of the photos were taken at the Blackberry Fair itself on the night of the incident. The first shows Kendes in Fortescue Lane about to climb the market's back wall. He is dressed in black with a rucksack slung over his shoulder. His face is pallid from the flash, his eyes two pinpoints of luminescent red like the tip of the cigarette dangling from his lips. The second photo was taken just over the wall inside the market. On either side of the photo, illuminated by the flash, are crude stalls lining the narrow laneway. In front of one stall is a church pew, on top of which are piled a number of wooden boxes. Vague shapes can be discerned in the deep background where the lane disappears into blackness. Only the nearest shapes can be identified from their outlines: wheel-less bicycle frames, the bell of an old gramophone; further in the distance is a human form that is probably the Virgin Mary statue. But it is the final photo that is the most curious. At first glance it is quite mundane. A pale and slightly blurry hand takes up most of the foreground. The hand belongs to the photographer, who can be identified by his wristwatch as Rex Liebl. He is pointing, finger then still attached, at something in the darkness beyond. There is some disagreement over exactly what Liebl is pointing at. Some see indistinct and unrelated shapes that they attribute to the market's rubbish-heap topography. Others, however, claim to see the faint silhouette of a figure. Fewer still describe with conviction what they believe to be a man wearing a long coat and a rounded hat.[23]

The fact that Liebl, Kendes and Ensine had been attacked and killed by rats caught the attention of the Health and Safety Authority, who promptly acted. Health inspectors determined that the fair, along with the houses numbered 40, 42 and 44 which the market's proprietor also owned and had packed full with detritus, had become a breeding ground for hundreds if not thousands of rats and other vermin. There has not been a major rat infestation in the city since the early eighteenth century, and there is no excuse for a preventable epidemic to exist in the modern day – not even in Dublin.[24] The market did not open that weekend and the courts saw to it that it never opened again. The time of

[23] The photographs in question were leaked to the media and printed in an article by John Reppion: 'Where Goes the Blackberry Man', *Ghostwriter: The Amateur Ghost-Hunter's Journal*, 62, August 2003.

[24] '*Walsh's Impartial News Letter*, 16 May, 1729, contains the following curious item of news: 'This morning we have an account from [south Dublin] that a parcel of these outlandish Marramounts which are called Mountain Rats who are now here grown very common … walk in droves and do a great deal of mischief.' The account then goes on to relate how these mysterious pests devoured a woman and a nurse-child in Merrion, and that the inhabitants 'killed several which are as big as Katts and Rabbits … This part of the country is infested with them. Likewise we hear from Rathfarnham that the like vermin destroyed a little Girl in the Fields.' (Joyce, p. 31).

the ghost-hunters' demise was judged to be between 9.24 p.m. (the time stamp on the last photograph) and 10.30 p.m. The coroner decided that 'Exsanguination secondary to multiple wounds inflicted by the common rat (*Rattus rattus*)' was the easiest way to catalogue the deaths of three otherwise healthy young men. But the old wives of Rathmines knew better: the Blackberry Man was to blame.

I was introduced to a fellow by the name of Osborne Brocas one evening at Slattery's pub. Unlike those who believe in the Blackberry Man only as a local spook story, Brocas has witnessed the phantom with his own eyes. Although I had never met him until that night, I had seen him around town and in Slattery's, so I knew of his reputation. Brocas is a painter of no small skill. One of his paintings even hangs in the Hugh Lane Municipal Art Gallery. He specialises in Dublin street scenes and cityscapes, past and present, realistic and fantastic. Until the Blackberry Fair closed, he sold his work there from a small and cluttered gallery that he and his wife ran at weekends. When my companion told Brocas that I was interested in the Blackberry Man, his smile straightened and he nodded solemnly. No, he did not mind talking about the night in question, but preferred to do it from the privacy of the snug.[25] 'It's not the sort of thing a

---

[25] A tiny space at the end of the bar partitioned from the rest of the room by wooden screens; sometimes called a confessional thanks to its privacy and direct communication with the barman.

man wants overheard in common company,' he said.

I bought a Smithwick's for myself and an orange juice for Brocas, who had told me, 'I never indulge'. And then he began:

'It was late summer. The market closed at six and sunset wasn't for a while. The market's always in shadow because of the dome, so it's always hard to tell what time of day it is. Everyone else had left, but I was allowed to stay a bit longer so long as I locked up when I'd finished. I was searching through my canvases that night for a painting I did called *Judgement on Aungier Street*. A collector in Lisbon had seen it listed in a catalogue and wanted to buy it.

'Sure I'd heard of the Blackberry Man. Who hasn't? I think my aunt told me about him. She was a real ghost-story addict, so it was probably her. I didn't believe in him though, not even at that age, and when I signed the lease for the gallery I just accepted the dawn 'til dusk thing as a superstition. Superstitions die hard around here. Of course a clause isn't necessary. The Blackberry Fair after hours is enough to prickle anyone's nerves. There was always something off about the place, even before that night. It's not the sort of place I make a habit of visiting alone. But that night was different. I had to post that painting by the next morning.

'The time must have got away from me. Like I said, the dome blots out the sun, and unless you stop and listen for them, the town hall bells get blotted out too. Every so often I would look across the courtyard. It was always the same – the fewer people in the market, the more rats you'd see scurrying about.

'After a while I stopped to take a smoke break and heat the kettle. As I smoked I could see the Virgin, with her hands folded and eyes closed. I got the feeling that maybe she was praying for my sake. As I looked at her, a plump rat scurried right up the folds of her robe. I'd never seen anything like it. I'll bet those things could climb straight up a wall if they wanted to. It climbed all the way to the top of her stone head and sat on its hind legs. It twitched and watched me with those expressionless little eyes like tiny black marbles.

'That was when I sensed the presence near the wall by the church. At first I thought it was the silhouette of some old rubbish. Maybe a dusty old rug that some-one had rolled up and leaned against the wall. But it wasn't a rug. It was a man. My eyes must have gradually adjusted with the evening. I hadn't noticed it was long past dusk. My first thought was that it was the proprie-tor come to turn me out. But instead the man just stood there.

'He was about fifteen or twenty yards away. His back was to me. He wore a long garment, like a Prince Albert frock that went down past his knees. And I think he was wearing a bowler. I've seen old photos of people from just before the First World War – my grandfather used to dress the same way when he was a young man. But this thing, it wasn't human at all. It was stiff like a coat rack and twitched like a rat. I remember how I didn't want it to turn around.

'Then three loud bangs, like gunshots, echoed through the market. I ducked behind a pile of canvases leaning against the wall. When I stood up, I saw the figure was doubled over on the ground. Its face was still turned away from me. Then it moved, contorting and pushing itself up with its arms. It twisted its torso at the waist. It turned and looked at me.'

Brocas closed his eyes. It takes resolve to conjure up and relive a frightful memory, even if only in the mind's eye. Brocas' voice trembled as he described what he saw behind his eyelids.

'Its face – it's horrible. I've tried to paint it since, but I can never seem to capture on canvas what's so vivid in my nightmares. Its face is like a blob of white oil paint polluted with streaks of grease and it glistens like melting wax. The eyes are deep hollows of nothing. It's sniffing at the air, but it has no nose. Its mouth is a drooping triangle, and it's dropping open, wider than any human mouth ever should. I can almost hear the hollow shriek pouring from its lipless mouth. It's dropped on all fours. It's crawling towards me.'

Brocas opened his eyes. His muscles were tense and

he gripped the bar, his arms ramrod straight, pushing his body against the wall. A piece of melting ice shifted and clinked in his glass.

'I didn't scream. I wanted to, of course, but I couldn't. Instead the instinct for survival welled up from deep within me. I knew I had to run. If I allowed that thing to get near, if it reached out with one of its pallid hands and clutched my ankle, I knew it would never let me leave the market.

'There were even more rats now, perched on every surface. Not a single corner was free from trembling whiskers and multiple pairs of evil eyes. And they were all fixed on me.'

Brocas knew how fantastic his story sounded, but before I could say a word, he propped his foot on a stool, rolled up his pant leg and pushed down his sock. His entire ankle and lower calf were covered with ragged scars where the rats had chewed through his trouser leg and nipped at his flesh. [26]

'My other ankle's the same,' he told me. 'Luckily the front gate was unlocked and I got through it in no time

---

[26] While swarms of rats attacking people may sound implausible, there are actually a surprising number of documented cases on record. After an informal search, the earliest account I was able to find dates back to 1850 when a horde of rats stripped the flesh from two *chiffoniers*, an ex-soldier and an old woman, who lived amongst the dust heaps in the environs of Montrouge outside Paris. One of the more recent reports is from Gates Falls, Maine, in 1978. Rats that had made their home in the sub-cellar of a textile mill killed the foreman and six nightshift workers who were clearing the old building. The lone survivor, Wisconsky, described not only an unnatural massification of rats, but also rats that had grown well beyond the average size.

at all. I'd hate to think what would have happened if I had to stop and find my keys. They probably would have nibbled clean through my tendon. I certainly wouldn't be here having this drink with you.'

The barman hammered the small brass bell above the bar and flipped the lights off and on as if trying to settle a classroom full of rowdy children. It was last orders, and people either bought another pint (sometimes two) or started to clear out.

'Have you talked to Molly Crowe yet?' asked Brocas, as he stood to leave. 'She's seen him too. After she met the Blackberry Man though, she left the market and refused to set foot in it ever again. Her spiritual awareness is – how can I put this? – more delicate than most people's. Last I heard she'd moved her stall to Blackrock.[27] Molly knows a lot about Rathmines; she grew up here. I think she still works one night a week at the coffee shop down the road. You might catch her there.'

The next Thursday I made my way to the coffee shop. A poster taped to the wall near the door read: MOLLY CROWE, PSYCHIC: PALMISTRY – TAROT – DIVINATION – €20. I found Molly seated at a secluded table in the far corner. My first thought on seeing her was of Maria Ouspenskaya, the fortune-teller mother of Béla Lu-

---

[27] If you wish to visit an approximation of the old Blackberry Fair, the Blackrock Market is still run every weekend in leafy Blackrock. Many of the vendors who used to trade at the Blackberry Fair relocated there.

gosi in *The Wolf-Man*. Molly looked the part. She wore lavender robes with a matching headscarf. From her ears dangled Egyptian scarabs, and a green knitted shawl hung around her shoulders. From an old carpet bag she removed the tools of her trade and arranged them on the table: crystals of all colours, a tarot deck and a crystal ball the size of a man's fist, which she placed on a yellow satin pillow.

I introduced myself. Without looking up she set the tarot cards in front of me. 'Cut the deck with your left hand.' I did as she said. 'Now – what do you wish to know?'

I explained that Osborne Brocas had referred me to her, that I was conducting private research on Rathmines, and about my interest in the Blackberry Man. Settling back into her wicker chair with a creak, she flipped over the top card. It was the Tower.

'The Blackberry Man?' She stared at me for a moment, perhaps deciding what she would or would not tell me next. 'I can see you're a healer. A true healer understands not only what he sees, but also what he hears.

'The fair,' she went on, 'always gave me a bad feeling, even as a girl when my mother used to take me there. It's a spiritually turbulent place. I wouldn't have rented a stall there, but times are hard and it was one of the few places where I could get one cheap.

'I set up my stall next to Brocas' gallery at the end of the row. I had a nice view of the courtyard from there. I remember it was a cold afternoon in late February of 2001 when I saw the Blackberry Man. He appeared to me clear as I am to you. I had no walk-ins or appointments that afternoon, so I passed the time with a crossword puzzle. 'Vito Corleone in *The Godfather Part II*' was the clue. Six letters. It's funny how you remember insignificant details like that. 'Brando' wasn't the answer, and I was about to go ask Madeleine Brocas for help when I saw a man hunched over near the Holy Mother. He had his back to me, but I could see he was digging in the earth with his bare hands like an animal. The market was mostly empty, and those who were walking about didn't seem to notice him.

'I watched for a few seconds before he rose from his knees. His arms hung at his sides. He wore a long coat and one of those hats that gentlemen used to wear. But this man was far from a gentleman. He sensed me, like an animal senses a threat. When he turned around I saw his horrible, thin-cheeked face. It was filled with contempt and rage. He grinned into my soul with his horrible hate-filled eyes. He pointed at me with a bony finger. I felt a burning sensation in my chest. I've had spirits enter my body before. It's like being mildly seasick. What entered me on that day made me feel violently ill.

'Then he started tracing letters on the air. As he wrote, I felt my own hand, the one holding the pencil, start moving about on top of the newspaper. I was writing what he was writing. When he finished he just stood there sneering. Then he turned and walked down the lane. I tried to watch him as long as I could, but something was wrong.

'I felt my clothes rustle. I looked down. My entire gown was alive, shifting and fluttering. Ropey tails whipped my body and a hundred tiny claws dug into my skin. "Get them off!" I screamed. I ran from the stall and tore the robe off, throwing it to the ground. I waited for streams of vermin to pour from my robe, but it only lay on the ground like a discarded rag.

'Madeleine Brocas rushed to help me. She was always a generous soul. She must have thought I was crazy, shouting and screaming the way I was. She helped me back to my stall and suggested I go home for the evening. I followed her advice, only not just for the evening. I knew I was never coming back to the Blackberry Fair.

'After she left, I lifted my shirt. I could still feel where the vermin had clawed me. I've never told anyone that before now. But I can sense you're a healer. My stomach, it was red and covered with scratches. There's also this.'

Molly removed a battered notebook from her bag. Paper-clipped to one of the pages was a folded piece of newspaper. When she unfolded it I saw it was a half-finished crossword puzzle. Scribbled on top in heavy capital letters were the words 'QUIS SEPARABIT'.

'It's Latin,' she said. 'I showed it to one of the curates at the church. He said it's from the Vulgate Bible. It means, "Who will separate us?"'

She handed me the notebook. On the same page that the crossword puzzle was clipped to was written 'Romans 8:35. *Quis nos separabit a caritate Christi?*' And below that: 'Who shall separate us from the love of Christ?'

Molly closed her trembling eyelids and put her hand to her forehead, which was now beaded with sweat. Her other hand blindly found the deck, turned over another card, and placed it beside the first. The Moon. Without even looking at it, she spoke: 'My advice to you is to stay away from the Blackberry Fair. Do your research, but do it from a safe distance. Any more questions? No? Twenty euro, please.'

A newspaper report, a painter and a psychic – what are we to make of their stories? We have a hat, so to speak, but no peg on which to hang it. These encounters with the supernatural might have remained incidental if not for an unexpected accident that drew them together.

The Rathmines library is not an uncommon place to find me. In fact, I conduct most of my research in the first-floor reading room. One particularly late evening, a helpful librarian brought me a stack of titles I had asked for about the Hell-fire Club. Somehow a book I had not enquired after wormed its way into the pile. The title was an interesting one, and since the librarian did not immediately come back to retrieve it for another patron, I figured there would be no harm in flipping through its pages.

The book in question was about the theft of the Irish Crown Jewels in 1907, a crime that sparks perennial interest here in Ireland, largely because it remains unsolved to this day. The aftermath of the theft, with its many accusations and dead-end investigations, is a confusing one. What I read was an admirable examination of the verifiable truths concerning this singular misdeed. I will do my best to distil for you the relevant details of the case. We depart Rathmines for the moment to visit the scene of the crime: Dublin Castle.

In 1831 King William IV bequeathed the Crown Jewels to the Illustrious Order of St Patrick, a chivalric organisation equivalent to Scotland's Order of the Thistle or England's Garter and Bath. William's father, the ever-unpopular George III, had founded the Order in 1783 in an attempt to reinforce the often wobbly relationship between Ireland and Great Britain. King George, however, failed to bestow ceremonial regalia to the fledgling order. William's gift of the Crown Jewels forty-eight years later resolved this oversight.

The Crown Jewels were composed of two individual ornaments: the Grand Master's Diamond Star, a sort of brooch, and the Diamond Badge, which was fixed to a decorative collar by *two tiny screws* (remember that) and worn around the neck. To give you an idea of their magnificence, the Badge is described on a reward poster as being: '3 x 2½ inches set in silver, with a shamrock of emeralds on a ruby cross, surrounded by a sky blue enamelled circle – with their motto "*Quis Separabit* MD-CCLXXXIII*" in rose diamonds, surrounded by a wreath of shamrocks – the whole surmounted by a circle of large single Brazilian stones, surmounted by a crowned harp in diamonds.' The Diamond Star is similarly described, and together they were valued at £30,000. This is considered a conservative estimate. Still, I dare not think what they would be worth today.[28]

The royally appointed custodian of the jewels at the time of their disappearance was Sir Arthur Vicars, head genealogist of the Office of Arms. Caring for the jewels was a duty of which Vicars was inordinately proud, and he was known to display them to the Office's visitors, particularly impressionable ladies. Until 1903, Vicars stored the jewels in a wooden wall safe in the damp and rat-infested Bermingham Tower in the castle's lower yard. When the Office of Arms moved to the Bedford Tower just beside the Cork Hill Gate, Vicars took the opportunity to have a new strongroom constructed to house the Order's valuables. The jewels were to be stored in the

---

[28] The reward offered by the Dublin Metropolitan Police for 'such information as will lead to the recovery of the jewels' was a mere £1,000. Given their total value, this hardly seems an incentive!

strongroom within a 'Ratner Patent Thief Resisting Safe'. However, due to a bureaucratic miscommunication, when the safe arrived the strongroom doorway was found to be too narrow for the bulky safe to pass through – or the safe was too wide, depending on which side you believed. A series of memos raced between the Office of Arms and the Board of Works, each side seeking to place the blame with the other. The problem was irreconcilable and eventually the safe – and its valuable contents – were discreetly placed in the Office of Arms' ground-floor library, near the corner window.

On the morning of 6 July 1907, Vicars lent his keys to the office messenger, William Stivey, so that Stivey might place some account books into the safe. This action was unprecedented. Never before had Vicars lent his keys to anyone, let alone the office messenger. He always removed items from or deposited them in the safe himself. Being only a messenger, and not wishing to invoke Vicars' stern treatment, Stivey did not question the task.

Stivey fitted the key into the safe's lock and twisted it. It refused to budge. He then turned the key the opposite direction and heard the latch click. When he tried to open the safe he found that, rather than unlocking it, he had instead locked it – that it had already been unlocked when he initially inserted the key. Stivey rushed to notify Vicars immediately. When Vicars arrived, he dropped to his knees and inspected the contents of the safe. He grabbed for the lock box that held the Crown Jewels. A look of utter alarm must have flashed across his face when he saw that the lid of the box was ajar. 'My God,' he shouted, 'they are gone! The jewels are gone!'

I suppose you can well imagine for yourself the panic that followed. Police Commissioner Sir John Ross arrived shortly thereafter, along with Detective Owen Kerr who, with the help of the other inspectors, searched the building, then questioned and re-questioned every member of staff. It was first established that neither the front door nor the safe had been forced, and so the thief must at some point have had access to the keys. But the strangest thing was the fact that the thief had removed the badge from its decorative ribbon collar – you will remember that it was attached with two tiny screws – and left it neatly folded in the lock box. Surely any thief who values his neck would spend as little time as possible at the scene of the crime. Why the thief spent the estimated minute and a half removing the badge from its collar is a mystery in its own right.

Detective Kerr asked Vicars if he suspected anyone. Vicars alone had sole responsibility for the jewels. His job was at stake and he almost immediately went on the defensive. The first person he singled out was Phillips, his coachman, whom he promptly dismissed from service. Phillips, he claimed, had access to the duplicate keys Vicars kept in his desk drawer at his home in Clonskeagh. The police summoned Phillips, and after thorough questioning established his innocence to their satisfaction. Six months later he was fully exonerated by the viceregal commission of inquiry. Embarrassed by the slanderous error that shattered his coachman's honour, Vicars paid for Phillips' passage to America, where he could begin a new life.

The second person Vicars decried was Francis Shackleton, feckless brother of the celebrated Antarctic explorer, Ernest Shackleton. As a suspect, Frank Shackleton had a number of strikes against him. He worked as a herald in the Office of Arms, and was therefore an unquestioned presence in the Bedford Tower. He also shared with Vicars the house in Clonskeagh and so, like Phillips, would have had access to the duplicate keys. Shortly before the theft, Shackleton had fallen into financial difficulties when he lost much of his money on a land deal in Mexico. His one saving grace was that he had been out of the country for a full month before the jewels were stolen. He had only returned to Dublin after the theft. With an alibi established, the viceregal commission eventually cleared his name from their list.

At about this time Vicars' own reliability came into question. Stories of after-hours parties held in the Office of Arms began to circulate around Dublin. Inevitably the commission turned its inquisitive eye on him.

Every newspaper and tabloid in Ireland and England reported the facts of the sensational mystery. Every man on the street had his own theory, and the police seemed desperate for one of their own. As with most highly publicised mysteries of the era, Sir Arthur Conan Doyle, perhaps guided by the Great Detective, offered his assistance. Although the Metropolitan Police politely declined, they curiously did accept the help of a local clairvoyant, who made the audacious claim that her spirit guide knew where the jewels were hidden.

Commissioner Ross and Detective Kerr were both present at the séance. The clairvoyant placed the safe key in the centre of the table, closed her eyes and went into a trance. 'Where will we find the jewels?' she intoned at measured intervals. Her hand began to move, her pencil scribbling on page after page. This went on for half an hour. The commissioner's patience wore thin. Just as he rose to leave, the candles flickered and a low, disembodied groan filled the room. 'Where will we find the jewels?' repeated the clairvoyant. The moan intensified and deepened. The clairvoyant's pencil scribbled faster, and letters began to appear in the scrawls: 'MIN MIN DED R AT MINE DEAD MINES.'

'Who are you? Show yourself!' shouted the commissioner as he threw back the window drapes. The moaning stopped; the clairvoyant slumped forward, hitting her head hard on the table. The light was bright enough for everyone to see the clairvoyant's face. It glistened scarlet red, shredded by a series of thin scratches. She was moved to a couch and someone went for a doctor. When the doctor arrived, he revived her with smelling salts. 'The jewels,' she struggled to whisper, 'they're hidden in a graveyard in Rathmines.'

On Sir John Ross' order, Detective Kerr hurried to Rathmines. When he arrived, he found the township possessed no cemeteries; the nearest burial ground was Mount Jerome in Harold's Cross. Though undeniably startling, the whole matter was swiftly hushed up by the already embarrassed police force.

Eventually both material and psychical leads were exhausted. The viceregal commission of inquiry adjourned without a conclusive verdict, but they did request a resignation from Vicars. Disgraced, Vicars quietly retired to his home in Kilmorna, County Kerry. On the night of 15 April 1921, a company of IRA men knocked on his door. Feeling that Vicars had been too sociable with the local British officers, they set fire to the house and dragged Vicars out to the lawn where they shot him in the head. Vicars' body was found the next morning propped against a tree as if made to watch his own home as it burned. Around his neck hung a sign: 'Traitor'. Field mice had already begun to nest in his pockets and feast on his body. The eyes were the first to go.

Even in his final will and testament Vicars maintained

that Shackleton was guilty. 'I was made a scapegoat to save other departments responsible,' wrote Vicars. '[T]hey shielded Francis Shackleton, the real culprit and thief (brother of the polar explorer who *didn't* reach the South Pole).' Eventually Shackleton was arrested in Portuguese West Africa in 1912 for defrauding a bank. Before he was informed of the charges, he said to the arresting officer in an apparent reference to the 1907 theft: 'Vicars owes me. That was the deal!' In early 1913 he was sent to Mountjoy Prison; when released five years later he was destitute and outcast. By 1914 he is listed in *Thom's Street Directory* as living at Welton Lodge, a gentleman's boarding house in Rathmines, where he offered his heraldic skills to the general public. An ad he placed in *The Irish Times* read: 'Antiquary and Genealogist. Pedigrees traced. Coats of Arms painted or engraved. Welton Lodge, 44 Fortescue Terrace, Rathmines Road.'

A lengthy summarisation of the Crown Jewels theft was published beside Shackleton's obituary in 1941. The landlady who ran the boarding house had found his body. 'He was seated in that chair by the window, like he always was, day and night,' she said. 'I never had any trouble with him. He was ever a gentleman, but the poor man always seemed like he was carrying some great burden.' Shackleton's rooms were at the back of the house, and his sitting-room window afforded him a clear view of the Blackberry Fair.

As with most of my obsessions, I read every book I could find on the subject of the Irish Crown Jewels. One of the worst I encountered was by an author whom some of you may already be familiar with: Harrison Bews Jr[29] Bews is known in the industry as a coat-tail author. He writes any book that will sell based on the short-notice success of other publications. His books are poorly researched, written in haste with an eye for deadlines and profit margins and titled to please retailers. In many of his books he is audacious enough to pass off spurious inventions as fact. In addition to countless volumes about the Freemasons, Bews has produced no less than three books on the Whitechapel Murders, each one identifying a different suspect 'conclusively' as Jack the Ripper. You get the idea. Bews' books are not to be recommended.

Shortly after Myles Dungan's excellent recounting of the case, Bews published his book entitled *Solved! The Mystery of the Irish Crown Jewels*.[30] It is a muddled account that contradicts itself from page to page. Naturally, Bews offers his usual array of theories: everything from the Freemasons' involvement with the theft to Jack the Ripper's. Still, in the name of thoroughness

---

[29] Harrison Bews Jr is the son of the respected paranormal investigator, Harrison Bews. The elder Bews is famously known for his investigation of the Grand Pavilion Theatre in Seabourne, England. See the *Journal of Paranormal Research*, Vol. X, No. 9 (July 1975).

[30] Myles Dungan. *The Stealing of the Irish Crown Jewels: An Unsolved Crime* (Town House, Dublin, 2003).

I slogged through it. You can imagine my surprise when I was rewarded with a curious detail I had not yet come across.

Bews' central pieces of 'undiscovered' evidence are a classified Dublin Metropolitan Police report written by Detective Owen Kerr and two brief memos, one by Kerr and the other written by Police Commissioner Sir John Ross. All three are dated 24 February 1909. Bews goes on to claim that 'an anonymous clerk at the Garda Archives' supplied him with copies of the documents.[31] I have searched for references to these files, if not the files themselves, but all my visits to the archives ended in failure; the 'anonymous clerk' maintains his silence. Here is a summary from the relevant chapter from Bews' book: At around 10 p.m. on the night of 24 February, Mr McBride, the landlord of Welton Lodge, summoned Police Constable Kelly after hearing three gunshots from the Blackberry Fair. When P.C. Kelly arrived, McBride assisted him in gaining access to the market. McBride fetched a lantern so that the two of them might make an inspection of the premises. Near the southern wall, adjacent to the church, they discovered two fresh corpses, one lying slightly on top the other. The man on top, who was wearing a bowler and a frock coat, had his hands wrapped around the other man's throat. He had been

---

[31] *An Garda Síochána* absorbed and replaced the Dublin Metropolitan Police in 1924, shortly after Ireland gained independence.

shot once through the forehead and twice in the chest. The strangled man was lying on his back, eyes still protruding with surprise, his mouth agape in horror. In his right hand was the revolver that fired the three shots. Between the bodies and the statue of the Virgin Mary was a trail of blood. The statue itself was spattered with blood, and a substantial pool had accumulated at its base. When P.C. Kelly realised a double murder had taken place, he secured the area and contacted his superiors at Dublin Castle.

Detective Owen Kerr arrived forty-five minutes later. He surveyed the crime scene and then proceeded to inspect the bodies of both men. He determined that the man with the revolver was probably German; a patch sewn to the lining of his jacket read: *H. Löher, Schneider, Bad Münstereifel.*[32] The inner pocket of his jacket contained a single ferry ticket to Holyhead, and in his trouser pocket was £8,000 sterling.

Next, Kerr inspected the man wearing the bowler hat. He found the man's hands were dirty and fingernails caked with earth. In one pocket Kerr found a neatly folded piece of tissue paper. In the other, he very nearly overlooked two tiny screws caught in the threads at the bottom of the pocket. With growing suspicion, he hastily wrote the following dispatch to Commissioner Ross:

---

[32] *Schneider* is German for tailor. Bad Münstereifel is a town in the Eifel region of Germany.

'Dead man in Rathmines resembles jewel suspect *Phillips*. Request permission to contact Inspector Kane at Scotland Yard. Kerr.'

He received a swift reply from Ross: 'Denied. Return to Exchange Street at once.'

Commissioner Ross' terse response is puzzling and seemingly obtuse. His failure to recover the Crown Jewels in 1907 was still a sore point between the Dublin Metropolitan Police and King Edward VII. Anything that reminded the public of Ross' shortcoming would only lead to further embarrassment. And given the increasingly volatile relationship between Ireland and the British crown – remember, at this point the Easter Uprising was only seven years away – Sir John Ross must have felt compelled to classify the report and keep the murders from further public scrutiny. This seems to have worked. I have yet to locate any contemporary newspaper articles concerning the double murder.

Kerr's noticeably muted report concluded the following: the man in the bowler met the German to sell 'an object or objects of great value'. The two men argued over the price. In anger, the German shot the other three times with his revolver, probably with the intention of taking the valuable object from the dead man. However, the object, whatever it was, was not found on either of the two bodies. Kerr determined from the blood splatter that the man wearing the bowler must have been shot near the statue. And given the amount of blood that had soaked into the ground at the foot of the statue, he must have died on the spot.

What Kerr does not explain, possibly on orders from Ross not to delve too deeply, was how the man in the bowler hat, who fell dead at the foot of the Virgin Mary, crawled the distance of fifteen metres, and then strangled the man who shot him. I shudder even to consider the notion implied by this.

Obviously we must take Bews' unsupported evidence with a grain of salt. Besides, by the final page, his book makes no real assertions anyway. Still, in the light of my own research, the facts on offer, and how they might relate to the Blackberry Man, are tantalising. The implied question remains: Did Phillips conceal the stolen jewels somewhere in the market before his fatal meeting with the German? And would the Blackberry Man take an interest in you if you sought the answer? *Quis separabit?* Who will separate us? I do not think I care to find out.

As I was passing by the old market the other day, I noticed a 'SOLD' sticker taped over the 'FOR SALE' sign which described the property as having 'OBVIOUS DEVELOPMENT POTENTIAL'. For days, workers carried an endless stream of scrap metal and broken furniture from the long-vacant buildings and lots the fair eventually came to encompass. It is little wonder that so many rats made their homes there. Will the broken windows trimmed and the padlocks taken off the doors? Whatever the new owner intends to do with these houses, we know two things for sure: number 44 will always be 'in the way', and the Blackberry Man – whatever it is – will forever haunt the folklore of Rathmines

Lavender and White Clover

You will have already noticed, as we came over the bridge, one of the most recognisable features of the Rathmines skyline. In fact, you can see it even from as far away as the foothills of the mountains, or indeed from any point within Dublin that elevates you well enough above the city. I am, of course, referring to the Byzantine copper dome of the Church of Mary Immaculate, Refuge of Sinners. From my desk near the window, I can see its egg-shaped curve, circular windows and stoic cupola even as I write this. Most people already know that this dome was the church's second to stand above the treetops of Rathmines. Here is what happened to the first dome.

On the morning of 26 January 1920, a great con-flagration nearly destroyed the entire church. The flames crawled up the walls, melting the stained-glass windows, and weakening the edifice; the weight of the dome could not be supported. It crashed down through the roof into the nave. The noise it made when it smashed into the ground, 'like a hammer striking some great bell', was even heard by the fishermen in the bay.[33] The new dome was constructed in Glasgow and it would have been shipped to St Petersburg had not the October Revolution broken out in 1917. Fortunately for the Scottish dome-maker, it was possible to give it a home here. But as I said, most people already know this story. Allow me to tell you some things about the church that you may not know.

The church that you see now is the latest of three to stand in this general area since the late eighteenth century. Following the Catholic Relief Act of 1782, the Parish of St Nicholas Without on Francis Street, of which Rathmines was a part, purchased a large parcel of land from the Earl of Meath. According to records, the property measured '2 acres 2 roods and 38 perches'. This piece of land roughly corresponds with the area defined by the Grand Canal to the north, Mount Pleasant Avenue to the east, Richmond Hill to the south and Rathmines Road to the west. Unlike today, the land had not yet been built upon. Its only residents were the (now subterranean) Swan River, which trickled from west to east

---

[33] An acquaintance of mine, Dr Donnelly, who is ninety-six years old (and probably even older by the time you read this), has lived in Rathmines all his life. He remembers quite clearly the day of the great fire. I am sure he will tell you about it himself if you buy him a whiskey. He also knows an interesting story about W. B. Yeats, but I will leave that for him to tell.

down the centre of present-day Richmond Hill, and an ancient Celtic cemetery which had existed since before recorded memory and was occasionally, even then, still in use.

A temporary church was built beside this cemetery with plans to build a larger, more permanent structure as soon as funds could be raised. However, these plans were dashed until 1823 by continued opposition to Catholic emancipation. Eventually a parish was established, and in 1830 Archbishop Murray consecrated the newly built, Gothic-style church to SS Mary and Peter. The Catholic population of Rathmines continued to grow, and as soon as 1845 the church was already too small for its congregation. Parish priest Fr William Stafford[34] hired noted architect Patrick Byrne to prepare plans for a larger church.[35] Fr Stafford envisioned a Greek cruciform church built on Richmond Hill; this latter specification he repeated to his successor, Fr William Meagher, on his deathbed in 1848. The parish planning committee adopted the cruciform design, but rejected Fr Stafford's Richmond Hill wishes. They declared that: 'they would

---

[34] A memorial detailing the life of the Very Reverend William Stafford (1768–1848), Rathmines' first parish priest, can be found in the south transept of the present church. He was a noted theologian and folklorist.

[35] The enigmatic architect and alchemist Patrick Byrne (d.1864) was educated at the Royal Dublin Society School and went on to design numerous celebrated Dublin churches. He is known for his impassive and mausoleum-like designs, often planned to fit constricted urban spaces. His churches include St Audeon's on High Street and St Paul's on Arran Quay.

be ashamed to have the House of God thrown into the background, which a century ago might have answered well for the little crouching Chapels of a trampled race, but was unfit for the present day and the structure now in contemplation.' Instead they decided to build the church facing Rathmines Road, just south of the old cemetery. In order to fund construction costs, most of the land acquired by the church in 1782, including the cemetery, was sold to developers.

Before building his terrace to the north of the church, Mr Fortescue had the cemetery's bodies exhumed and relocated to Glasnevin along with the grave markers. The disinterment progressed without incident until one of the workers discovered a deposit of loose stones three feet beneath the surface of an unmarked plot. The discovery caused some excitement and before long the workers had excavated the stones and uncovered a plain coffin half a length longer than most standard coffins. As two of the workers hoisted the box, one of them lost his grip. The coffin splintered open to reveal the well-preserved body of a man who measured an astonishing seven and a half feet. Fr Meagher was quickly summoned, and the mummy, for it was said to resemble the similarly described corpses in the vaults of St Michan's, was examined.

The unclothed body had been lying face down in its coffin. Its ankles were bound with a piece of twine that had been dipped in wax. The waxen twine still held strong and showed no sign of decay. There was no indication of when the man had been interred; no record of such a burial could be found in any known archive.

When the workers turned the body over they found that the features of the man's face, though extraordinarily pallid and sunken, were still distinguishable. According to *The Freeman's Journal*, he was 'possessed of an aquiline nose with strangely arched nostrils, his chin broad and strong. Thin tresses of white hair, fresh and untangled, grow from his head as if recently sprouted'.[36] Strangest of all was the man's mouth, or rather what was stuffed in it. As the startled workers looked upon their discovery, crossing themselves and muttering prayers, the corpse's still red lips parted, as if exhaling. The sudden change in atmosphere must have spurred decomposition, for gravity continued to pull at the jaw until it rested against the corpse's throat. The mummy's mouth, gaping like its own disturbed grave, had been packed full with sprigs of lavender and white clover.

Fr Meagher observed the proceedings, entering every detail into a notebook. Before the ink had had a

---

[36] Some literary scholars believe that Charlotte Stoker, mother of *Dracula* author Bram Stoker (1847–1912), related the details of this ghastly discovery, widely reported in Dublin at the time, to the young boy. Charlotte relished telling the child morbid stories, and Bram's description of the infamous Count is curiously similar to those in contemporary newspaper articles about the Rathmines mummy.

chance to dry, he hired a carpenter to build a new coffin, specifying that it be made of oak. He then gathered up fresh clover and lavender, and carefully re-stuffed the mummy's mouth. He made sure that the waxen twine was still well knotted. To this he added a complex knot of his own with the leftover length. The lid was fixed into place with iron nails. The coffin was then returned to its hole, dug now even deeper; the stones replaced, and the earth packed level. Fr Meagher presided over a private ceremony, the details of which he did not record. But we do know that the ritual concluded with the erection of a statue of the Virgin Mary over the site where the tall man was, and most likely still is, buried.

After the peculiar incident with the mummy, there were no further delays in the construction of the new terrace. Likewise the church was finished according to schedule. When it opened in 1856 it was 'Dedicated to God the Most High, under the invocation of Mary Immaculate, Refuge of Sinners'.[37] The imposing portico, with its smooth Portland stone columns, handsomely carved Corinthian capitals and statue-adorned pediment, was added in 1881, the year in which our next story is set.

---

[37] This is inscribed in golden letters on the portico's façade: '*D.O.M.*' (*DEO OPTIMO MAXIMO*), and below that '*SUB.INVOC.MARIÆ.IM-MACULATÆ.REFUGII.PECCATORUM*'.

Father Corrigan's Diary

If you speak the name of Father Corrigan in the presence of most schoolchildren, you are likely to be met with the same groan of bored disinterest that an adult might wish to utter while standing in a queue at the local post office. Indeed, along with similar banes such as maths, history and Irish, *Father Corrigan's Diary* forms part of the curriculum for several south Dublin schools. The book is similar to Father Nathaniel Burton's *Letters from Harold's Cross* in that it provides an insightful, if quaint, account of daily life in late nineteenth century suburban Dublin. Schoolchildren, no doubt, have other more immediate concerns. A single-page biographical blurb at the front of the 1972 Irish Classics edition of *Father Corrigan's Diary* tells us the basic facts of the curate's life:

> Father Simon Corrigan, the only surviving son of an illiterate bootmaker, was born in Meath Street, Dublin on 1 August 1840. His elder twin brother died at birth. A

physically weak child, Corrigan possessed no aptitude for cobbling, but showed an early gift for reading and writing. At the age of fifteen, the precocious adolescent entered the Roman Catholic College of Maynooth where he began keeping a record of his daily life. His first diary entry is dated 24 February 1858, two years before Archbishop Cullen assigned him to the sacristy of St Nicholas Without. These early entries detail ecclesiastical life at a time when Catholicism was still gaining political and economic influence in the wake of the Roman Catholic Emancipation Act of 1829. When Corrigan was thirty, he was made curate of the Church of Mary Immaculate, Refuge of Sinners in Rathmines, Dublin. Corrigan was acquainted with many of those who influenced the growth of south Dublin, including Rathmines town commissioner, Terence T. Dolan; Sir Howard Grubb, proprietor of an astronomical instruments firm; and the Hanna family, who are to this day still in the book selling trade. Many thought that Corrigan would succeed Dr William Meagher as the next parish priest of Rathmines, but in 1881 Corrigan unexpectedly retired from the curacy. He lived the remainder of his life in a sanatorium in Glendalough, County Wicklow where he died on 12 October 1882.

Not a detailed summary, but I hope you get a sense of who Father Corrigan was. The book is composed of a selection of the more interesting entries ranging from 1858 to 1880, and has not been out of print since its first publication in 1922.[38] The original handwritten journals, a total of fifty-two volumes, are currently

---

[38] The first edition was published to help recoup expenses incurred by reconstruction after the 1920 fire. It was edited and introduced by Canon Mark Fricker, and published by Hanna & Sons in 1922.

housed in a dusty corner of the presbytery library of Mary Immaculate. I came to read the manuscript diaries through the generosity of the current curate, who apologised for their shabby condition. 'It's been a good many years since anyone's gone through them,' he told me. 'There's always been an interest, but I'm under the impression that the curates who preceded me were hesitant to accommodate researchers on the grounds that everything of interest is already in the book. Still I see no harm in letting you have a look.'

Soon the curate departed and left me alone in the small and uncommonly dim library. A large gilt-framed mirror hung over the fireplace. Presumably this was placed to create the illusion that the room was more spacious than it was in actuality. Ironically, I felt even more crowded as I now shared the room with another researcher, working silently in the room opposite. And whenever I glanced up to steal a look at him, I would find him already watching me.

I set about examining the journals piled on the desk before me. The binding had begun to fall apart on some, and many of the pages showed signs of foxing and mould. Father Corrigan's thin sepia scrawl made for difficult reading, but with persistence I soon had it mastered. There are many aspects to Corrigan's life that have not formally been made public. The only one that concerns us here is that, although the book's final entry is dated 28 December 1880, Father Corrigan continued to write through 1881. After reading these later diaries, it is easy to understand why the editor chose not to incorporate them. As far as I can tell, the 'unexpected retirement' mentioned in the biographical note was prompted by a gradual nervous breakdown from which Father Corrigan never recovered.

The events leading up to Corrigan's breakdown are interesting, and I could not justify closing the covers, re-shelving the diaries and ignoring what I had read. With no small amount of pleading, the curate reluctantly permitted me to transcribe some of these later entries. He agreed to this only on the grounds that my audience is a small and discerning one. And so it is to you that I submit further extracts from Father Corrigan's diaries:

Monday, October 3rd, 1881

Dust! It is inescapable and sometimes I feel as if a fine grit fills my nose and mouth and parches my throat. It is almost as if we are being buried alive in it. The taste of earth is always on my tongue.

This afternoon Fr Sheridan and I accompanied Fr Meagher on his perambulation of the building site.[39] As usual I attempted to dissuade him from the inspection. He once ran quick as a lamplighter but is now-a-days less ambulatory than he was even last year, and is often after

---

[39] Father Thomas Sheridan was the sacristan of Mary Immaculate from 1876 to 1881.

slight physical exertion short of breath. Sometimes I fear he shall not be long with us. Nevertheless, he takes great pleasure in observing the portico's progress. He introduced me to Mr Byrne whose work I greatly admire.[40] Mr Byrne pointed to the newly erected pediment with his walking stick: 'There will go St Laurence, and there, on the other side, St Patrick. In a few weeks time we shall move St Mary to her proper place at the apex, but first we must bring her down to be cleaned.'

I was eager to inspect Mr Farrell's work on the Madonna up close, and commented so to Fr Sheridan, but my comments went unheard.[41] A man as tall as Fr Sheridan is not difficult to spot. I spied him on the other side of the courtyard surrounded by a small group of workers. Judging by their rapt attention, Fr Sheridan was weaving some grotesque tale or entertaining with some new-found scrap of folklore, both of which he is fond of in equal measure. I believe he has been feeling out of sorts these past weeks. Nothing pleases him more than telling tales, and it is good to again see even a weak smile on his lips. And so I left him to his stories while Fr Meagher asked Mr Byrne questions about stone-cleaning techniques and the placement of the invocation on the face of the pediment.

After Mr Byrne departed, Fr Meagher told me once again how much it will please Canon Stafford to see the new church finished at last. Stafford has been dead these past thirty-three years, but Fr Meagher speaks of him with increasing frequency as if he were still with us. I never had the honour of meeting the Canon, but have often seen his stony face and pupil-less eyes in the south transept memorial. I sometimes feel as if I know him. As if he were but away on a long journey and his return is soon expected.

---

[40] W. H. Byrne, the architect who designed the portico. Not to be confused with Patrick Byrne, who designed the church.

[41] James Farrell was the sculptor who carved 'Our Lady of Refuge'. Fr Collier purchased the statue for the church at an 1853 exhibition in Dublin. SS Patrick and Laurence are also Farrell's handiwork.

This evening brought me no small amount of pleasure. After the evening meal I went for a short walk to visit my kittens at the rear of the church. They are still five in total, and grow healthier by the day. I am delighted with the hope that they will some day mature into hearty felines. It has been two weeks since I discovered their den behind the overgrown privet growing near the back wall, where they huddle together out of reach. There is still no sign of their mother and I fear that they are now entirely orphaned.

As has become my habit, I placed before the bush a saucer of fresh cream and some scraps of fish, and backed away some fifteen paces. I expected the same thing this evening as in the past. I would wait, sometimes feigning to inspect a window or some other feature of the church, and hope that the food would lure the kittens from their den so that we might become properly acquainted. Normally I give up after ten minutes and return to the presbytery, but on this evening the black cat emerged from the bush sniffing the air with great timidity. 'Hello,' I said to him quietly. He raised his head and looked at me, not knowing whether to proceed or retreat to safety. I realised my mistake and said no more. 'Blackmouse' – that is what I now call him – turned his attention back to the saucer and soon lapped at it hungrily. I waited for his brothers – or sisters, for I know not their sexes – to follow suit, but none is as brave as my 'Blackmouse'.

Saturday, October 8th, 1881

Fr Meagher retired to the presbytery early this evening after complaining of chest pains. I offered to fetch the doctor but he assured me that the pains would pass if he sat and rested for a while.[42] He patted my shoulder, reached

---

[42] From 1850 until 1962 the presbytery was located at number 52, the first house in Berry's Terrace to the south of the church. The front door of number 52 faces the church courtyard. In 1962 the presbytery was moved to the end house of Fortescue Terrace on the opposite side of the courtyard where it still stands today.

for his stick and exited the church. Unbeknownst to him, I stood at the doorway and watched him cross the short distance between the church and the presbytery, ready to offer assistance should he need it. I nearly rushed to his aid as he negotiated the steps, but Mrs Maguire appeared in the doorway and helped him inside. I returned to the vestibule to finish unpacking the new hymnals.[43]

When I finished with my task, I went into the nave to make my final rounds, secure the exterior doors, &c., &c. before leaving for the night. Before doing this, I dimmed my lamp and allowed the echo of my footfalls to dissipate into the emptiness of the dome. It is at times like this, when the Lord's house is dark and serene, that I feel as if there are no obstructions between God and His creation. Often I stand in the cavernous silence and allow my eyes to adjust to the moonlight streaming through the dome windows. To-night this solitary moment was brief. I was startled to find that I was not on this night alone in the church when a figure emerged from the dimness of the south transept.

I do not know how long he had been standing in the recesses for he made no sound during my moment of introspection. Nor did I hear the south door open and close, which it never does without an unharmonious complaint from its hinges. I could see from the outline that the man was tall and thin, and wrapped in a sort of heavy cloak or blanket the colour of soot. My first guess was that this was Fr Sheridan returned from his engagement, although why he used the south transept entrance, or why he was even in the church at this hour, I was unable to guess. 'Hello,' I called out to him. On hearing my voice, the figure halted before the side-altar and snapped its cowled face towards me. I half expected for it to vault at me over the many rows of pews that separated us, but it attempted no such feat. The side-altar's candles flickered behind it, and I fancied

---

[43] A cook and general servant at the presbytery, Mrs Maguire is mentioned peripherally throughout *Father Corrigan's Diary*, but little else, not even her forename, is known about her.

that the votive light even shone *through* its towering frame, as if the figure were but a dense vapour. Without reply, it continued to move in a manner of haste, crossing the altar without pause for genuflection, a profanity which Fr Sheridan would never have committed, and entered the sacristy through the Gospel-side door. Through all this I was astonished that his footfalls made not a single sound.

I adjusted my lamp and brightened the church as best I could. I hurried to the south transept, gave the exterior door a tug, but found the lock was already secure. I then crossed the front of the church, same as the figure, and approached the Gospel-side door to the sacristy. The door was ajar and the room beyond was dark. I do not know why I called Fr Sheridan's name, for I neither expected nor received an answer. I pushed the door open and thrust the lamp through. Before entering the room I carefully watched for the figure to exit the sacristy by the Epistle-side door on the opposite side of the apse. I entered the room confident that the man must still be in there, but I realised soon after a brief search that I was alone. There was not a trace of a single living soul. My heart rate calmed, and I believe I even laughed with relief.

The blame for my fright rests firmly with Fr Sheridan. Two months ago he lent me the first volume of a collection of stories by an American journalist, whose name I have successfully banished from memory. I tried to read it, but threw it down after the third tale, some nonsense about a man who murders himself. The stories were truly monstrous. I do not know how Fr Sheridan delights in grotesque horrors, or indeed how anyone can open their inner eye to the possibility of such dreadful encounters. They have a tendency to play on the imagination with the sole aim of burdening the reader with sleepless nights. Even now, a full two months after my brief reading of these tales, my nightmares are still inspired by imaginary bugbears.

The only thing that I could find amiss in my inspection of the sacristy was a cassock that had somehow found its way to the floor. The crumpled white linen was saturated with wine from a bottle that had tipped onto a nearby table; scattered across the table's surface were fragments of the sacramental host. I sought no further answer to this mystery than rats. The construction of the portico has disturbed their nests, and I fear a good many have sought refuge in our church. I am all the more eager to befriend 'Blackmouse', who I am sure will be happy to assist with this issue. I cleaned the mess as best I could and left the rest for the morning.

After securing the church, I returned to the presbytery. Fr Meagher had already retired to his room, and Mrs Maguire, after making me a pot of tea, closed the pantry up tight, and left for the evening. Fr Sheridan was seated in his usual chair by the fireplace reading a book when I entered the drawing room. Despite sitting so close to the fire, he had wrapped himself from head to toe in a thick blanket. I asked him how his dinner went with the Irish Photographic Society, his third such social engagement this week. Fr Sheridan is a most popular dinner guest and Fr Meagher believes his storytelling, no matter how perverse, is in part responsible for inspiring a good many donations for the portico. 'I left early,' he told me. 'I was feeling unwell.' I sensed something weighed heavily on his thoughts. I went to his side, placed my hand on his shoulder, and asked if I could be of any service. 'If it is no trouble, would you move the lavender into my bed-room? I think I shall retire soon.' He had brought his ubiquitous vase of fresh lavender from his bed-room to the parlour, and had placed it on the table beside him. I did as he asked and decided not to further bother his oc-cupied mind with the sacristy business. I will tend to that myself to-morrow.

Sunday, October 9th, 1881

Fr Sheridan looked better this morning, but still spoke very little. Mrs Brenane caught my arm after Mass today. She told me how pleased she was with the new hymnals and commented on the continued progress of the portico. 'I will be thankful when the construction is done,' she said. 'With so much mud I have ruined nearly all of my good dresses and soon I shall have none left!' I believe she would have continued on in this way had not Mr Grubb waved for my attention.[44]

Mr Grubb took me aside and made sure of our privacy. He enquired as to the health of Fr Sheridan explaining that he left the gathering rather abruptly last night. I put down here Mr Grubb's words as best I remember them from this morning: 'During pudding last night we asked Fr Sheridan to tell us one of his stories. As usual we were captivated by his tale. I hope one day he will write them down and send them to the *University Magazine*.[45] Just as we were about to find out to whom the great uncle's cursed mirror originally belonged, Fr Sheridan paused in the midst of the tale, and his face took on an expression of great horror. You know yourself how Fr Sheridan often animates his features whilst telling tales, and so we thought for an instant that this was part of his game. We soon realised that he was in a sort of trance, and his horrified gaze was fixed upon the window behind us. Something gave my eldest daughter Ethel an awful shock when she turned and looked. She shrieked and fled the room. My wife went after her. I looked at the window, but only saw Fr Sheridan's tortured expression reflected in the pane. When I turned back, Fr Sheridan had already risen from the table and was standing by the dining-room door. Mr Kinsella urged him to lie down, but Fr Sheridan assured us that this was not necessary. He did the most peculiar thing before he excused himself and left: he requested fresh

---

[44] Howard Grubb, later Sir Howard, was a telescope designer and proprietor of the Grubb Telescope Company. He was knighted by Queen Victoria in 1887.

[45] *The Dublin University Magazine* ran from 1833 to 1877. It was renamed the *University Magazine* in 1878 and was published under that title until 1882. Joseph Sheridan Le Fanu was the *DUM*'s editor from 1861 to 1870.

lavender. My servant brought him a sprig of it from a bundle hanging in the kitchen. He took this and pinned it to his jacket. You can understand my concern, Fr Corrigan. I was relieved to see him on his two feet during Mass this morning; I do hope he is all right.'

By this time Mrs Brenane had wandered to within earshot of our conversation, and so I shifted the topic to the improving health of Mr Grubb's eldest son, Howard. He scarcely had time to respond before Mrs Brenane approached us, hooked Mr Grubb's arm in her own and led him to the courtyard to acquaint him with her thoughts on the portico. Despite her outward sociability towards Mr Grubb, I do not believe Mrs Brenane holds him in very high esteem since he joined our congregation two years ago. Hardly a Sunday passes that I do not observe Mrs Brenane furtively scowling at Mr Grubb, only to see this scowl shift to pleasantries when his attention turns to her. I suppose I shall never understand what conflict Mrs Brenane holds in her mind.

Even the best of moods lighten when Fr Whelan visits to take our confessions from us, and then afternoon tea with us.[46] Fr Whelan's snow-white hair and wrinkle-framed smile have always reminded me of my grandfather. Judging from his general popularity, I imagine others feel quite the same. I am told that he is older than Fr Meagher by a number of years, but he still carries on as if half my own age. However, this afternoon was gloomier than usual, not leastwise from the low hanging clouds that threatened to burst all afternoon. Fr Meagher was lively in Fr Whelan's presence, though still noticeably drained. After updating Fr Whelan on the progress of the portico, Fr Meagher retired to his room asking not to be disturbed for the remainder of the afternoon. Fr Sheridan was likewise distant and spent

---

[46] Fr Alfred Whelan was the chaplain of Portobello Barracks, not far west of Mary Immaculate. In 1922 the British military handed over the barracks to Gen. O'Duffy and Comdt Gen. Ennis of the Irish Army. Today it is called the Cathal Brugha Barracks.

most of teatime by the window reading a book with an indecipherable title in German of which I later made a note: *Aufsätze zu metaphysischer Medizin.*[47] Occasionally Fr Sheridan would comment on our conversation, but mostly he kept to himself and his attention on the book. He too excused himself to his room shortly after Fr Meagher, and soon Fr Whelan and I were alone. 'He looks poorly,' noted Fr Whelan after the subject of his comment left the room. I confirmed his suspicion, and although I wanted to tell him the little that I know, I felt I should not elaborate. I hope Fr Sheridan will volunteer the details in his own time. Instead I changed the subject to my hallucination in the church on Saturday night. 'The clouds passing in front of the moon used to unnerve Fr Stafford too,' he told me. The creases around Fr Whelan's mouth deepened into a reassuring smile. I did not join Fr Whelan to-night on his evening constitutional. Many things weigh upon my mind at present, and I should like some time alone with them.

Monday, October 10th, 1881

My kittens are in good health and are not showing any weaknesses of the world that surrounds them. Mrs Maguire teases me by calling them my silly animals. 'I don't know why you encourage them,' she tells me. 'We are all God's creatures,' I told her. 'Besides, they will some day make good catchers of rats.' 'You make a fair point, Father,' she said, 'the dust has stirred up a good many of them marramounts these past months.'

The kittens are more trusting of me now, and of the world in general. They provide me with a few moments of mental ease each evening when I visit them. When I

---

[47] I had much trouble finding bibliographic information for this book whose title translates into English as *Essays on Metaphysical Medicine.* The German physician, Dr Martin Hesselius, wrote it and the book had a limited print run from a small publisher in Heidelberg in 1794. It has never been translated.

bring them their food I stop worrying about Fr Meagher's health and Fr Sheridan's secret troubles. I went outside tonight with food, and they were already padding around the yard near the privet. As always, when they caught sight of me they scurried for safety, all of them except for my Blackmouse. Tonight he stopped short of the bush. I sat down on the ground, placed the cream in front of me and tapped my nail against the saucer. We watched each other for almost half of an hour. I called to him, gently chirping and speaking in soft tones. He slowly approached me. A rush of joy filled me when soon he was dipping his pink tongue into the cream. I feared the pounding of my own excited heart would send him scurrying back to the bush. When he had had his fill, I reached out and touched his shiny black fur. He did not flee, but instead pushed his head into the palm of my hand and emitted a satisfied purr from deep within his throat. At long last I picked up my Blackmouse and placed him in my lap. He continued to purr and never once struggled. One by one, as if called by my brave Blackmouse, the other kittens came out to drink from the saucer.

I feel foolish now, and I admit only here that I must have dozed in my contentedness. By the time I awoke it was quite dark and the kittens had silently crept away. I could see nothing in the darkness, but as I rose I heard the branches of the privet rustle softly. No doubt my kittens settling in for the night. I write these words wrapped in a blanket, with an ache in my neck of my own doing. Though the hour is now late, any sense of weariness seems far distant.

Saturday, October 15th, 1881

The presbytery was in a state of commotion when I returned from visiting my family in Glasnevin this evening.[48] Fr

---

[48] Presumably Fr Corrigan means visiting his family's grave in Glasnevin Cemetery. The funerals of both his father (d. 1864) and mother (d. 1873) are noted in earlier diary entries.

Sheridan, with his gaunt face even gaunter, was pacing in front of the drawing room fire and fidgeting with his key ring. Seated in a chair was a man I did not recognise, but who soon introduced himself to me as Detective Montague. His associate, P.C. Nolan, busied himself scribbling in a note pad at the desk in Fr Meagher's office. They had been awaiting my return. Fr Meagher was nowhere to be seen.

When I entered the room, Mrs Maguire bustled over to me and took my coat. 'It's terrible, Fr Corrigan, just terrible!' she said. Det Montague explained that a significant sum of money had been stolen from Fr Meagher's office earlier this afternoon. Not only was one month's collection taken, but also a sizeable donation for the new portico given by Mr Grubb two weeks ago.

There are three keys to the office. In addition to Fr Meagher's, Fr Sheridan and I each retain copies. Det Montague asked if I still had mine. I removed the key ring from my belt and let him examine it. He asked me if I ever lent it to anyone. I replied in the negative. Satisfied, he returned the key and informed me that Fr Meagher and Fr Sheridan were also still in possession of theirs.

Det Montague offered me a seat and then called for P.C. Nolan. Taking the note pad from the constable, he read for my benefit Fr Meagher's statement:

'I had been doing some light work in the sacristy all morning,' said Det Montague, speaking Fr Meagher's words. 'Fr Sheridan was dusting one of the side-altars.' To this Fr Sheridan nodded in affirmation.

'I cannot say why, but I felt as if someone was watching me. Indeed, when I turned around, Fr Sheridan was standing in the doorway of the sacristy. He was silent and seemed to have been observing me as I worked. "I don't suppose you could fetch the ledger from my office?" I asked him. He smiled rather sharply, an expression I had never seen on him before, and set off without speaking a word.

'After a quarter of an hour Fr Sheridan returned empty handed. "Did you not find it?" I asked him. "Find what?" he replied. "Why, the ledger, of course. I asked you to fetch it for me some fifteen minutes ago." "My apologies, Father, I did not know you wanted it. I have been occupied cleaning the side-altar this past hour. It occurred to me only now to check in on you." And Fr Sheridan rushed off again to fetch the ledger.'

As I listened to Det Montague read from the note pad, my gaze met Fr Sheridan's. He was standing by the window absently knotting a stem of lavender. He had been watching my reaction to the statement with an air of curiosity, or what might have even been unease.

Det Montague continued reading, this time from Fr Sheridan's statement. When Fr Sheridan reached the office, the door was already ajar. In the lock was a key, and when he twisted it, he found that it turned the tumblers perfectly. Instinctively his hand went to his belt for his own key, which he found to be safely in its place. He entered the library, worried, but not yet alarmed. When he discovered that both the ledger and money were missing, he alerted Fr Meagher. Shortly thereafter the police were summoned. Until I arrived, they expected for the key found in the door to be mine, a notion I dispelled when I produced my own copy.

Det Montague handed me the fourth duplicate key to inspect. It had all the same characteristics as my own. Had mine not been attached to my key ring, I certainly would not have been able to tell them apart. 'It was likely made from an impression,' Det Montague explained. 'The thief must have somehow stolen a key, had a copy made, and then returned it as secretly as it was taken.' As to the identity of the robber, not so much as a hint was forthcoming. Not a trace of the intruder could be found.

Mrs Maguire was away at market the entire afternoon. She saw and heard nothing, but received a shock to learn that an intruder might at some point have been lurking about the presbytery while she was still in it.

Fr Sheridan is determined to blame himself. Although he offers no proof, he is certain that his own key served as the original for the perpetrator's copy. I fear this will do nothing to cheer Fr Sheridan's gloom-stricken humour.

Perhaps most affected by the robbery was poor Fr Meagher. After answering Det Montague's questions, he retired to his room and had already requested privacy by the time I had arrived. I did not wish to disturb him. What comfort could I possibly bring? Like Fr Stafford before him, the church is his very being, and although I did not speak with him to-night, I know the severity of the disaster wracked his fragile constitution.

Monday, October 17th, 1881

Fr Whelan led Mass yesterday morning, and is cheerfully content with taking on the extra duties until Fr Stafford's health improves.[49] However, his condition is worse than we feared.

He is too weak to rise from bed and has not spoken to anyone since the robbery. The deep sleep from which he rarely wakes is plagued with restlessness. We take turns sitting at his bedside and watching over him whilst beads of sweat break upon his brow. When he is awake he communicates with frail gestures if he is hungry or thirsty, otherwise he remains lethargic. It is all we can do to feed him thin porridge and change his linens when necessary. It breaks my heart to see him suffer so. He has worked so hard for this parish. If he is soon to be called to his reward, then I pray that he lives long enough to see the completion of the portico.

Tuesday, October 18th, 1881

Fr Sheridan is increasingly solitary and anxious. The slightest tap or squeak of the floorboards now causes him

---

[49] Corrigan obviously meant to write 'Meagher' here, not Stafford.

to recoil with dread. Yesterday morning I found him in the presbytery library searching the shelves for a book. His back was turned to me when I entered. I did not think twice when I placed my hand on his shoulder and began to speak. His reaction startled me as much as my presence frightened him. He stumbled backwards, pulling violently from my touch as if it were not my hand, but that of some unwelcome fiend; with his other hand he clutched at the sprig of lavender pinned to his breast. His terror only passed when he recognised me. A look of embarrassment and apology crossed his face, but even then with hints of cautiousness. I knew an explanation would not be forthcoming. I have since taken to announcing my presence from a distance with undue clatter so as not to startle him.

Fr Meagher's room is now filled with the perfume of fresh lavender. This morning Fr Sheridan brought in a vase and placed it on the windowsill. He also hung a bundle bound with a short length of twine from a nail above the bed-room door. Mrs Maguire told me in confidence that she finds the smell overwhelming, but Fr Sheridan's absolute conviction in rural medicines forestalled further comment. I once asked him about his affinity for the plant. His grandmother, a Sligo woman, always put lavender in his room when he was ill he told me. 'She said it aids in the spirit's respiration.'

Although we are all grateful to Fr Sheridan for his devotion, we spend much of our time persuading him to heed respite lest his own constitution fail irreparably. Until then he is determined to spend his every spare moment keeping watch at Fr Meagher's bedside.

Wednesday, October 19th, 1881

A most horrible thing has happened. My hand trembles at the very thought. I can barely bring myself to put down in writing my frightful discovery.

This evening I made my daily trip to the rear of the

church to visit my Blackmouse. I tapped the saucer as I approached, expecting my kittens to bound forth from their den, and rub their sleek bodies against my legs purring with anticipation. But not a single one of them came. They are older, growing braver by the day. They must be exploring, I thought, hunting their own dinner, or already ridding the church of rats. I tapped the saucer again, more firmly, and again I waited. When still they did not come, I approached the bush, pushing away its branches and peering into the shadows. I could just barely see my kittens there, in a shallow depression near the wall, huddled together in a mass of black and white fur. Were they but sleeping, exhausted from sport? The lump that began then to grow at the back of my throat remains with me even now as I write this. I chirped at them, and still my kittens did not move.

Mrs Maguire answered my call. She brought a light from the kitchen and held back the branches so I might crawl closer to the kittens' secret den. The branches protested my admittance. They scratched at my hands and face, but I continued to crawl towards the heart of the bush, my face acquiring a new skin of spiders' webs. Soon I was within an arm's length of their den. I reached out my hand and placed it on the nearest kitten. He did not stir, and I all too horribly realised that this once living creature, so affectionate and warm, was now lifeless and cold. Its form was rigid and unresponsive to my touch.

How can I write so when I can barely bring myself to think it? My kittens are *dead*. Their glossy fur now bruised sacks of smashed bone. They did not die at the jaws of some feral beast, for their skin showed no sign of scratches or blood. No, it was something far worse than animal. They were suffocated and crushed by the *hands* of some heartless beast with a *cruelty* of the lowest order. When I close my eyes I can see their glassy eyes, claws protracted, and teeth bared in a defiant hiss against their executioner. Mrs Maguire did not dare look as I removed their cold bodies from the depths of the bush. 'Who is capable of such a deed, Father?' asked Mrs Maguire. I did not, or rather could not, answer her.

Such are times as these when one's heart is weighed heavy by limitless despair. But the bodies that I removed from the bush were only four in number. There were *four*, not five! My heart grasped at hope when I realised that my Blackmouse was not among them. Did he escape? Was he watching me from a distance? I took the bodies of my dead friends to the adjacent field at the rear of the church, and dug a hole not far distant from the Swan River. I prayed that they would rest easy. And all the while I kept an eye on the tall grass for my world-wary Blackmouse. Will he ever trust me again?

My hand and heart are aquiver. I cannot continue to write.

Thursday, October 20th, 1881

A dark shape loomed at the foot of my bed when I awoke this morning. I hardly knew whether it was an apparition left over from my nightmares, or if my room had been invaded by some horrible presence. With my bed-room located at the north of the building, I get precious little daylight, and the overcast sky saw to it that not even a ray of sun passed the curtains of my murky little room. I reached for my eyeglasses on the nightstand, but the shape was bold, even against lucidity, and did not dissipate in the seconds it took for me to recover my senses. I was relieved to find that the dark form belonged to Fr Sheridan, but my relief was replaced with concern when my eyes focused on his countenance, one that I can barely describe with adequacy. His face was pale and his lips were pulled back in a hideously wide smile. 'Are you all right?' I asked him. 'Is there something wrong?' He did not reply. I tried again. 'How is Fr Meagher this morning?' I asked. He still did not answer, but rather turned himself on the spot until he was facing the door, and after covering an impossible distance

with two long strides, he was through it. I listened for the
hall floorboards to groan under the weight of each footfall,
but they never once uttered in displeasure.

I quickly dressed and went into the hall, expecting to
find Fr Sheridan waiting for me, but instead I found it
empty. The door to Fr Meagher's room was open and I
paused to look in on him. Fr Meagher was lying in bed
with the linens pulled to his chin. He was in a deep sleep.
I watched his chest rise and fall with his usual laboured
breathing. The chair beside the bed was empty, though
Fr Sheridan's book lay open upon the nightstand. As I
stood in the room, I noticed that the scent of lavender was
absent for the first day since Fr Meagher took ill. Seeing
that nothing was amiss and everything was in its place, I
continued down the hall.

The next room I passed was Fr Sheridan's. His door is
usually ajar during the daytime, but on this morning it was
shut tight. Only a thin sliver of light passed between the
bottom of the door and the floor. Normally I would not
attach significant meaning to a closed door, but as I passed
this one I was startled by what sounded like a muted yowl
emanating from within the room beyond. I paused before
the door and held my breath, though I did not realise I had
ceased breathing until I was quietly gasping for air. The
yowl tapered into silence, and it was not long before I heard
the shuffling of feet. I called out Fr Sheridan's name, but
received no reply. Nor did I get a response when I knocked
gently on the door. The shuffling stopped instantly as soon
as I had made my presence known, and I was left to wait
in silence.

'Good morning, Fr Corrigan,' said Mrs Maguire when
I entered the kitchen. 'I've just come down to make Fr
Meagher his porridge. Are you off to help Fr Sheridan? He
was up early this morning, you know. Said he had business
in the church. Still not looking well, I should say, but I did
manage to feed him before he hurried out. You look like
you could use a nice breakfast yourself, Father.' I politely
declined as many times as necessary. I had not eaten since

yesterday evening. My mind was restless, and as is often the case at times like these, my belly felt full. It was on the tip of my tongue to tell her that Fr Sheridan was not in the church, rather he was upstairs in his room, though after the business last Saturday I did not wish to upset her by implying that someone got by her careful watch without her noticing.

The vase of lavender that had been in Fr Meagher's room was standing in the centre of the kitchen table. 'I had to remove those,' Mrs Maguire told me as she touched the tip of her nose. 'Had me wheezing like a consumptive. You will not tell Fr Sheridan, will you? It would only upset him. I promise to put them back in a bit.' I agreed not tell, and after reassuring her again that I was not hungry, I left the presbytery for the church.

I crossed the courtyard and waved to some workers who were just arriving for the day. There were fewer workers to-day as construction of the portico is nearing completion. All that remains is some minor finishing, to raise Mary Immaculate to the apex, and then remove the scaffolding. The last of the dust should settle over the next few weeks and we shall spend most of our time removing debris from the church's corners.

What happened next sticks in my mind, and no amount of logic has yet reconciled it. When I entered the vestibule of the church I was surprised to find Fr Sheridan, whom I had heard not five minutes earlier bustling about in his room. But here he was before me, covered in dust, broom in hand and hard at work sweeping the final heap of debris into the dustpan. Yesterday the vestibule was an insurmountable mess, a task that would have taken a single man the better part of the day without break to accomplish, and to-day it was without so much as a muddy footprint. 'You are awake, Fr Corrigan,' he said, surprised. 'I thought you might sleep into the afternoon. I was unable to sleep myself, so I thought I might get an early start on the vestibule. I have been at it all morning.'

As he spoke, a most terrible thought crossed my mind, and I must have gone visibly pale at the notion. 'Do sit down for a moment, Fr Corrigan.' But Fr Sheridan was the one who needed to sit, for his body wracked with a coughing fit when I told him that an intruder might be in the presbytery.

Together we raced to his room, startling Mrs Maguire as we flew past her on the steps without word. The door to Fr Sheridan's room was still closed, and when he twisted the knob he found it to be locked. He seemed puzzled, and I did not ask him then whether he had locked it himself. Using his key, we entered the room without further difficulty. We were met by absolute disarray. Fr Sheridan's usual clutter of papers had been scattered and shuffled about, dumped from their folders and loosed from their bindings so that not a single patch in the room was uncovered; the towers of books that sprouted from the floor had been toppled like Babel; and the vase of lavender lay smashed below where it once stood on the windowsill. The window was wide open, and I overheard Fr Sheridan quietly scolding himself for not having closed it.

Fr Sheridan spent the remainder of the afternoon sorting through his scattered effects, a chore that will occupy him for a week if not two. There are questions that I still cannot resolve, and will ponder into the night. Surely I would have seen or heard Fr Sheridan leave the presbytery this morning had he done so while I was speaking with Mrs Maguire. If Fr Sheridan were inside, then how could he have finished the not trivial task of cleaning the vestibule? And what caused his papers to be strewn about in such a way? Fr Sheridan attributed this to an open window, but the air was calm the entire day without so much as a light breeze.

17 Leinster Sq.
Mon., Oct. 24

Dear Father Corrigan,

We are in terrible sorrow. Our eldest boy, Howard, has been taken from us. I have already told you the long story of his ill health & the operations he had to go thru'. On the night Father Sheridan visited 2 weeks ago Howard was feeling better & even well enough to sit upright in bed & speak briefly with him. By the following Monday Howard's condition worsened & for this last week all doctors had given him up. The doctors call it lung disease but I do not trust in their verdict. On Sunday night Howard's temperature went down so low that no clinical thermometer would register it. This morning again the temperature went down & by noon our dear boy was taken from us.

Father Sheridan had been a comfort by visiting each afternoon with fresh lavender to brighten Howard's room & by praying with us. It had come to a point where we hardly knew whether to pray for Howard's recovery or his release. Thank God however he no longer suffers in pain.

Yours sincerely,
Howard Grubb[50]

Tuesday, October 25th, 1881

There is still dust everywhere. Fr Meagher's fever broke, and though he still remains unconscious, he no longer needs constant observation. We are now able to spend more time performing our churchly duties. We dust statues

---

[50] I found the above single-page letter with a heavy black border wedged between the entries for Thursday, 20 October and Monday, 25 October..

in the side-altars and wipe the windows. On some windows the dust is sometimes so thick that the little sun we do get is virtually blotted out. It is tiring work, and as Mrs Brenane said, we shall only be glad when the construction is finally finished.

Fr Sheridan is still unwell, but the excess work he takes on thankfully does not erode his health further. And he has certainly not shied from his duties. I see him tending to Fr Meagher just as often as I see him about the church. If idle hands are the devil's playthings, then Fr Sheridan need never extricate himself from infernal persuasion.

This evening I will visit the Grubbs. I hope I can be of some small comfort in the loss of their son. Fr Sheridan has volunteered to sit with Fr Meagher until my return.

Sunday, October 30th, 1881

Mrs Maguire's scare on Friday is not to be overstated judging from the enduring effect it will have on her.[51] Though truth to tell the precise details of what happened are still a mystery to us all, save for Mrs Maguire and, perhaps, Fr Sheridan. What we do know with certainty is that Mrs Maguire, with her customary discreetness, now refuses to be alone in the same room as Fr Sheridan. Even with others present, she avoids direct or lengthy interactions with him. She refuses to enter the church now too, though she made an exception for Mass. Thankfully she still continues to serve us in the presbytery with admirable fortitude. I have tried to speak to Fr Sheridan, but he shows a reluctance to talk with anyone on private matters these days. Mrs Maguire

---

[51] Fr Corrigan is referring to an incident that occurred on 28 October; however, Fr Corrigan made no diary entries between Tuesday the 25th and Sunday the 30th. What scared Mrs Maguire and exactly how Fr Sheridan was involved is left purely to speculation.

has not spoken with me about the incident, and to my knowledge made no attempt to engage Fr Whelan this afternoon.

Monday, October 31st, 1881

To Mrs Maguire's unpleasant incident I am afraid I must now add one of my own. Like what Mrs Maguire suffered, the episode I am about to recount, even now, seated here at my bureau in the familiarity of my room, fills me with a dread. Unlike Mrs Maguire, the gravity of my experience dictates that I must alert Fr Whelan if we are at all to preserve Fr Sheridan's well-being. I will record what I saw and heard if only to be clear in my own mind, although I do not think that I risk forgetting something so horrible. The entire morning seemed to me uncanny, and so I shall start at its beginning.

The baptismal font had been neglected for several weeks, as we have had no cause of celebration to use it. This morning I found myself in the south transept tending to the build up of dust that clung to every ornament of the font's surface. Fr Stafford watched me from the memorial on the north wall, his eyes, like the font, covered with a film of grey residue. With the aid of a step-stool I elevated myself to the same level as the Canon's stony visage. Damp cloth in hand, I wiped the dust from his eyes. The unsoiled brightness of the bone-white circles on his ashen face burned with strange intensity such that filled me with unease. Fully neglecting the font, I tended to Fr Stafford's other features, wiping his brow and cheeks, and making the collar of his shirt white once again. As I cleaned the words that recounted the good deeds of his life, the cloth slipped from my fingers and fluttered to the floor. Upon returning to my perch I made a startling discovery, although I hesitate to call a detail as such when I must have previously overlooked or misjudged the detail in question. Fr Stafford's face was no longer facing straight ahead, as it was in even my most immediate memory, but was now angled slightly towards the east, so that I fancied his gaze rested upon Fr McCarthy's memorial.[52]

Fr McCarthy's piety and virtue have long been of great inspiration to me, and the inscription from Job writ upon the stone is likewise writ upon my heart. 'The ear that heard him blessed him, and the eye that saw him gave witness to him.'[53] Often in my duties I have seen the image at the bottom of the memorial. It depicts a ship caught in the stormy waves of the bay in which Fr McCarthy drowned. I find it illustrative as much as I do allegorical, and often I have meditated on its meaning, seeking refuge in Fr McCarthy's memory. Today, as I looked upon the ship's impending fate, a peculiar phrase entered my thoughts: *Navis fluctibus devorata, navis flammis devorata.*[54] Why such a thing should enter my mind, I cannot say, but I did not have time to consider its provenance for I was interrupted by the sounds of a door opening and someone entering the church.

I quit my mundane task, eager to offer assistance to this unexpected caller, yet when I entered the nave I found the church to be quite empty. Not even the votive candles flickered and disturbed the unbroken stillness. Yet I was certain someone was present, and when I again scanned the room I spied a faint movement in the north transept. It was the penitent-side door of the confessional, and it was being

---

[52] I have visited Mary Immaculate on many occasions, and Fr Stafford's face is indeed 'angled slightly towards the east' as described in the diary. Like Fr Stafford's memorial, Fr Simon McCarthy's can still be seen. I have not been able to trace Fr McCarthy's birth, but his tragic death is recorded on the memorial: 'Revd Simon McCarthy, / Several years curate of this parish / who perished / in the wreck of the Rothsay Castle Steam Packet / in Beaumaris Bay, on the night of / the 17th August 1831.'

[53] Job 29:11

[54] Latin for 'A ship engulfed by waves, a ship engulfed by flames'. The waves depicted in the memorial indeed bears a striking resemblance to flames; I do not think Father Corrigan's comparison is a surprising one.

pulled gently shut. I knew of no confession scheduled to-day, and my puzzlement was further compounded when I began to wonder how anyone could have spanned the considerable distance from the vestibule to the confessional in such a brief time. Of course I had no intention of skulking, but the stealth of my footsteps attested otherwise, and I soon found myself drawn nearer the confessional. My suspicion of a visitor was confirmed when I heard a man's voice speaking in low tones within the stall, and although I could not make out individual words, I could hear the anonymous penitent muttering his constant and fevered confession with hardly a pause to breathe. The strained whisper made my own throat ache with hoarseness.

I confess that I was acting out of curiosity when I decided it was then time to dust the pews in the nave. Fetching the cloth and bucket, I took a position at the end of the church opposite the confessional, where I crouched down low and began dusting the nearest bench. Despite my sincerity at the time, I admit now that I positioned myself in a way that afforded a clear view of the confessional, though whoever emerged from it would not have the same view of me.

After a wait that could not have been more than five minutes, the confessional opened and the penitent emerged. He left the church in the same swift and determined silence in which he had arrived, and he did so at such an astonishing pace that I scarce had time to identify the *unmistakable* shape of Fr Sheridan. At long last, I thought: 'He did heal them, and from their destructions He delivered them.'[55] I sat in wait for Fr Whelan, for the confessor could have been no other. I had by then decided to speak with him about Fr Sheridan's health, but for as long as I waited, the confessor's door remained closed.

When I could wait no longer, I approached the confessional. I tapped the panel on the confessor's door, but the dark wooden stall yielded only hollow echoes by

---

[55] Psalms 107:20

way of response. My concern, unfounded though it was at the time, grew by degrees to the point of frenzy. There was little I could do to control myself, and when I could no longer endure the anxiety, I flung the door open wide.

Tiny bits of torn paper, fanned by the swinging door, whirled into the air and spilled forth onto the floor. I picked up a handful of these scraps and saw written upon them random words and numbers in Fr Meagher's own heavy script. This was, without doubt, what remained of the ledger stolen some two weeks earlier. But it was not this act of destruction that disturbed me most. The true evil was to whom, or rather to what, Fr Sheridan had uttered his confession – an inconceivable blasphemy, offensive to the sensibilities of both God and man.

The odour of putrefaction wormed across my tongue, and I nearly left the church for it. Upon the bench lay Fr Sheridan's mysterious confessor: a slender black shadow the length of a man's arm; one all too familiar to my heart's memory. Four tiny paws stretched and its stomach pulled taut as if in its final moments it basked in the warm sun; its sleek tail, bony and absent of once lustrous fur, still curled at its tip with unhesitating approval. I fled that church, now suddenly dark, and wept to remember the name I had once given my beloved companion.

Tuesday, November 1st, 1881

Fr Sheridan was nowhere to be found this morning, and secreted himself from prying eyes for the remainder of the day. When I arose early from a restless sleep, I already found him to be absent from the presbytery. His bed-room door was ajar; the bed appeared to be disused and the room showed no sign of recent tenancy, save for the ever-present fresh bowl of lavender on the window-sill. Its sweet fragrance, to which we are all accustomed, filled the room with its usual potency, but on this morning the odour elicited an unsettling notion. How, I wonder, or rather, *where* does one locate fresh lavender in the autumn months?

I toured the church and grounds with the partial hope of locating Fr Sheridan, but my lack of good fortune was merciful. Had I found him, would I dare approach him? Would I speak to this new stranger? Surely he knows I saw him in the church yesterday?

Fr Whelan arrived late this afternoon to visit Fr Meagher and sort through some papers. Fr Sheridan's absence proved beneficial as it provided me with the opportunity to speak with Fr Whelan in confidence. He sat at Fr Meagher's desk, myself seated before him, and I related the events of these past months culminating with the horror in the confessional, which I committed to these pages yesterday. He listened with sage-like concern, running his aged fingers through his ivory-white hair or lightly tapping a stack of papers at the story's more worrisome turns. When I told him about the fate of my Blackmouse a shadow of darkness overtook his face. Never before had I seen the reassuring calmness of Fr Whelan's face so disrupted by confusion and alarm. Twice he opened his mouth to speak, and twice the words retreated. Finally he spoke, though his words of comfort thinly veiled his more substantial and unshared thoughts. Fr Whelan assured me that he would invite Fr Sheridan to accompany him on his constitutional and speak with him then.

I sit here now at my bureau accompanied by the scratching of my pen. As I write, I can hear the floorboards in the hall groan under the weight of someone's careful tread. Fr Sheridan has returned, for if not Fr Sheridan, then who?

Wednesday, November 2nd, 1881

My brother once told me that it is always best to start at the beginning. If I write down to-day's events and examine them with the benefit of hindsight, perhaps I might be able to look upon the summation of their parts. Perchance a pattern, or some piece of hitherto overlooked *trivium* will suggest itself and allay my suspicions and unease. What is done cannot be undone, and we must all eventually meet our Maker. But Fr Whelan's drowning will still no doubt sadden many in our congregation. Even now I cannot accept that he is no longer with us.

Fr Whelan found cause to join us for dinner this evening, citing more work in Fr Meagher's office, though his true motive was to speak with Fr Sheridan. In his inoffensive way Fr Whelan suggested that he join him on the walk, and Fr Sheridan, without looking up from his dinner, calmly agreed. He even suggested that the brisk autumn air might invigorate his health. I do not think he suspected Fr Whelan's plans. Fr Sheridan excused himself from the table to finish packaging some chorister robes in the sacristy that we are sending to the Nativity in Chapelizod. After Fr Sheridan left the table, I had a brief word with Fr Whelan, and then also excused myself to finish some work in the church.

Once there I busied myself dusting the side-altar in the north transept. Not work that I enjoy, but work that must be done before the public unveiling of the new portico. Fr Sheridan was still working in the sacristy, and had not once emerged since I started.

I had long lost sense of the hour when Fr Whelan entered the church. The vestibule door startled me when it slammed shut behind him with an echo. 'I am starting off early,' he told me. 'I would like a chance to think. When Fr Sheridan is ready, please tell him to catch up with me.' I remember his next words exactly. They were the final words he ever spoke to me. 'I think to-night I shall walk east, along the south side of the canal towards Ranelagh Bridge.' I looked at my timepiece as he left. It was nearly nine o'clock.

All was quiet until fifteen minutes later when I chanced to look up from my work. I knew Fr Sheridan was in the sacristy, so I thought it odd to see him emerge from the unlit corner of the south transept, as I had not seen or heard him go there in the first place. I meant to call out to him and relay Fr Whelan's message, but Fr Sheridan glided across the nave in such a hasty manner that I wondered if I would have had time to recite the message at all. Even had I alerted this strange man to my presence, I still would not have been able to muster the boldness to speak to him.

With these thoughts swirling around my head I continued polishing. As I worked, the once cavernous dome began to feel close and restrictive, as if it descended on me like the bell of a candlesnuffer. Not much time had passed when I felt the weight of a hand resting upon my shoulder. I reeled around. I felt faint and almost crashed into the candles at the sight of my visitor. 'Are you all right, Fr Corrigan?' It was Fr Sheridan who asked this question. I had seen him leave the church not five minutes earlier, yet here he now stood before me. 'I thought you had already gone to find Fr Whelan,' I said as I swayed on the spot. He grasped my elbow and helped me onto a pew. When I regained my composure, I relayed Fr Whelan's message. 'He left without me?' asked Fr Sheridan with a look of concern. 'Perhaps you should go back to the presbytery. You do not look well. You will forgive me, but I must go.' He adjusted the lavender pinned to his coat, and then made his way to the vestibule; the door slammed shut behind him. I followed his advice two or three minutes later.

Mrs Maguire brewed a pot of tea and set me next to the fire. And that is where I sat for the next half of an hour with a rug draped over my legs to bar the chill. My eyelids had nearly shut when I heard a distant thumping on the door. Subsequently Mrs Maguire rushed in with a boy aged about eleven or twelve in tow. I recognised him as young Robert Harrison, son of the architect Mr Lloyd Harrison, who lives at number 1 Cheltenham-place along the canal.[56] He did not have to speak for me to know that

---

[56] *Thom's Dublin Street Directory* indeed lists a Mrs Harrison as living at number 1 Cheltenham-place during 1881.

something was horribly wrong. He shuffled on the spot as if he had been caught committing some roguish prank and then, bolstering his confidence, he said, 'Please, Reverend, my father says to come quick, I don't think he'll last much longer.' His vague message was troubling enough to greatly upset Mrs Maguire. I helped her into a chair and made sure she would be all right until I returned. Without so much as putting on my jacket, I raced down Rathmines-road as fast as I could. Young Harrison was already far ahead of me.

In the darkness the canal looked like a strip of shiny black ribbon. As I rounded the corner onto Canal-road, I saw a hunched figure standing between the two maple trees on the banks of the canal. I scarce had a chance to distinguish the shape of the figure from the surrounding shadows before young Harrison called to me from the top of the steps and gestured for me to follow him into the house.

Mrs Harrison greeted me in the hall. Her hands were red from constantly wringing them together. Three children huddled behind her, inquisitive of my arrival, but not daring to speak. The front hall carpet was wet and stained with muddy footprints leading from the front door to the drawing-room door, through which Mrs Harrison then ushered me. On the floor in a puddle of water and mud was the broken form of Fr Whelan. He lay at a peculiar angle, as if his torso had been somehow mangled. For only a brief moment I glimpsed his blue lips and his white hair clinging to his forehead. As I entered the room, a young man in wet clothing was pulling a linen sheet over Fr Whelan's body. Mrs Harrison closed the drawing-room door behind me, shielding the horrible spectacle from the innocent eyes of her children. Fr Sheridan sat in the far corner. His face was grief-stricken and cheeks streaming with tears. He did not acknowledge me or even look at me when I entered. His attention was fixed on the body that lay at the centre of the room.

'I am sorry we had to meet this way, Father.' This was Mr Lloyd Harrison speaking. 'My eldest son, Parry, heard Fr Sheridan shouting for help.' He motioned to the young man who was covering the body. 'It is most unfortunate, but Fr Whelan must have somehow fallen in. Luckily my boy can swim. We tried to revive him. I am sorry that there is nothing more we could have done. I tried to ask Fr Sheridan what happened, but he has not spoken a word to anyone since he got here. The poor fellow was near frozen with terror when we found him. My wife helped me coax him inside.'

Fr Sheridan did not respond to my questions. As Mr Harrison said, he was in a stupor and nothing I said shook him from it. Occasionally he gulped at the air, like a fish on land, as if he were drowning. At last he tore his gaze from the sheeted body and looked into my eyes. 'I was weak. I was terrified, Fr Corrigan, please forgive me. I failed to offer him absolution before he died. I watched him die and there was nothing I could do.' Then he unpinned the lavender from his jacket and pinned it to mine. 'Please, keep this with you.'

Mr Harrison had his man assist me in bringing Fr Sheridan and Fr Whelan's body back to the presbytery. To-night they both rest, Fr Sheridan sleeping in a deep fever, Fr Whelan sleeping his eternal rest. What am I to do? Fr Whelan is dead, and yet I still find myself fearing for the worst.

Thursday, November 3rd, 1881

This morning Fr Sheridan's health had deteriorated by noticeable degrees. Like Fr Meagher, he is now weak and confined to bed. This illness has plagued him for the past weeks and now it threatens to consume him. Is it an illness of the body? The mind? Or something else? I spent much of the day writing letters, including one to the caretaker of Prospect Cemetery and another to Archbishop McCabe.[57]

---

[57] Prospect Cemetery was the original name given to Glasnevin Cemetery on the north side of Dublin. This Catholic cemetery was founded in 1832.

Our situation is dire and we feel increasingly isolated here in our duty.

Mrs Maguire came to me in the office shortly after lunch. She informed me that Fr Sheridan was awake for the first time since last night's horrible events. He asked to speak with me. The air in his room was sour and thin. Mrs Maguire opened the window to let the fresh autumn air into the room before she left. The lavender on the window-sill was no longer fresh. It showed signs of wilting and its potent fragrance had already faded. Fr Sheridan was propped up in bed with pillows and he opened his eyes when I entered the room. For the first time in many weeks he seemed relieved to see me. I sat in a chair beside his bed and he proceeded to tell me his story at a whisper:

'After speaking with you in the church yesterday, I made my way to the canal. I hoped to meet Fr Whelan there. Rathmines-road was empty. I remember this because I saw hints of movement in every shadow, but never did I spy the man who moved. I walked filled with the hideous notions that I always hoped were confined to the written word. What if no one existed behind the shuttered windows of these vast terraces? Worse still, what if tenants unfamiliar pushed their fat white faces to the panes with the desire to inflict upon me their malign intent? Perhaps I am a fool, but in a bid to remove myself from these wicked dens, I walked the remainder of the distance down the centre of the road.

'Nor did I move to the side of the road when I reached the base of the bridge. But this bridge that I knew so well by day had become a great, slumbering beast hunched over the water, glutted on the bones of travellers. An omnibus might have sped towards me, advancing on the steep bridge from the opposite side at a deathly speed, and the driver would not be aware of me until he was at the peak, and the minute had already passed. And yet I stayed my ground.'

Throughout the story Fr Sheridan paused either to rest his eyes or while his body was wracked by a thick cough.

But now he closed his eyes and ceased talking completely. I waited patiently for him, wondering whether he might be asleep, and worrying that it might be something more. When he began to speak again his eyes remained shut, though he continued his story as if reciting the nightmare as it was experienced. I will commit to my diary the general course of his narration, but I cannot say what is real and what is the product of his feverish imagination.

'I stood at the intersection where Rathmines-road meets the Canal-road, and from here even in the moonlit darkness I had an easy view of the canal's southern bank. You will know the two ancient maple trees that stand not far from the bridge. Between the bank and these trees I saw the outline of Fr Whelan. He was poking among the rushes with his walking stick. As I watched, I felt as if a cold damp stone were pushing against my belly from the inside. I knew I was meant to witness a terrible disaster unfold upon this stage. I could think of nothing else to do than run to him; perhaps fate would choose me instead.

'Before I could intervene, a man I had not previously seen emerged from the shadow of the tree, or perhaps he stepped out of the trunk itself, I cannot say which with any certainty. I can describe him though, oh yes, how could I fail to have seen this demon? He was tall like me and thin like me, and his feet did not so much as rustle the dried leaves as he crept towards Fr Whelan. Fr Whelan suspected none of this and only saw me as I ran towards him shouting. But he scarcely had time to respond before the tall man shoved him into the canal. The man pushed with such strength, and Fr Whelan went into the water with such force, that I still wonder if he died from a broken back before he drowned.

'This demon, Fr Whelan's murderer, turned to me, Father, and in two steps it traversed the distance between us. When it emerged into the moonlight from the shadow of the canopy I chanced to look upon its face. I saw it, Father. Until then I had only suspected, but I have now seen him with my own pair of eyes. I cannot say where he came from or even why, but this fiend looked upon me only with malice and hate, and he did it not with his eyes, but with my own. I will continue to see that face, Father; in all of my daily reflections until my dying day, I will forever be forced to see that face.'

'Who was it?' I asked him. 'Who pushed Fr Whelan into the canal?' He looked at me with horror. 'I did, Father. Please forgive me, but it was I who did it.'

After this he would say no more, whether by choice or due to his increasing fever. I have spent the evening considering what he told me. Poor Fr Sheridan is haunted, though I know not by what; whether a spectre plagues his poor mind, or a fiend, as if from one of his tales, acts against him with horrible intention.

Mrs Maguire and I will do what we can while we wait for word from the Archbishop. If I do not receive word from him by tomorrow, I may travel to into Dublin come Saturday. I do not know how long we will last here otherwise.

Friday, November 4th, 1881

Had this been one of Fr Sheridan's ghastly stories, I would have thrown it down long ago. I would have pulled the sheets to my chin and knees to my chest, safe in the knowledge that the tale would remain confined between the covers of the discarded volume. But *this* book, with its tattered binding and yellowed pages, has forced my vision. It beckons me to look upon its words, to read its unthinkable implications and confuse my senses. Dawn is still many hours from us. I dare not leave the safety of my room, not even for the sake of Fr Meagher whom I have forsaken in his helpless state. What has become of him I cannot say, nor do I dare to think. I feel sick with wonder. God help me, I lack the courage and faith to throw wide the locked door of my room and read the book's final page.

Recording my thoughts in this account is all that I can do now to keep my mind from what lies beyond the door.

This is the paradox with which I continue to live. And yet how can the sober mind of man, in all its futility, ever hope to grapple with such awful events and emerge triumphant? One feels compelled to place them within the earth beneath our feet. But try though I might, I can comprehend no *meaning*, no *reasoning* behind the events I have recorded. Such are the machineries of Hell that catch the soul with its hooks and draw it ever in. Misery's demons need give no purpose.

The air in the confessional was stifling and almost too thick to breathe. I went there earlier this evening for the sake of those who sought absolution. I felt a safety in the darkness of the confessional, alleviating parishioners of their sins and absolving them of evil. Perhaps it was I who should have been on the other side of the screen, confessing sins of my own, instead of receiving them from others. Soon the stream of penitents ended, and I knew that the church beyond the confessional was empty. My mind churned and became swollen with thoughts of Fr Meagher and Fr Whelan, of Fr Sheridan and Blackmouse. Soon an unbearable weariness overtook me, and I must have dosed there in the solitude of the confessional, though I cannot say with certainty for how long. My next conscious memory was awakening in darkness to the sound of the stall on my left opening, a penitent enter and then pull shut the door. Slowly I raised the screen, and from the other side burst a most foetid odour such that caused my gorge to rise.

'Bless me, Father, for I will continue to sin.' The voice in the cramped stall beyond spoke with the whisper of a throat constricted. 'You know nothing, Simon Corrigan, but know this: only to you do I reveal myself and only in your presence do I confess all. Long have I desired you and all that is yours; all that you love, I have taken to crush and destroy as my own. Soon he too will belong to me. My time is long, Simon Corrigan, much longer than you could ever fathom in your limited being. I will not rest until the nave is engulfed by flames and this church is reduced to cinders. I have made this my duty. You may bless me, *Brother*

Corrigan, but know that it is I who damns you with this knowledge.'

His words hung in the air like an awful echo that refused to leave my ear. This impenitent monster's words filled me with a mixture of terror and disgust. Brimming with these emotions, and betraying the confidence of my office, I threw back the heavy curtain of my stall. The door of the left confessional was already ajar, and in this brief time, its occupant had already traversed the distance to the vestibule. How he accomplished this inhuman feat is unthinkable, especially when I recognised the very human face of he who performed it. The man who had whispered that perverse confession, and who was now exiting the church, was none other than Fr Sheridan, whom I believed was, at least earlier to-day, unable to rise from bed! My options were limited, and I could think of no other reaction than to give chase. Had I known then what I was chasing, I might have fled the church, if not the country of Ireland, forever.

I made my way across the courtyard and up the steps of the presbytery. Fr Sheridan had left the door wide open in the wake of his flight as if he were inviting me to follow. I first passed through the kitchen to beseech Mrs Maguire for help, though I know not what I expected her or anyone else to do. Perhaps I hoped she might somehow calm Fr Sheridan's madness. I know now that this would have been futile. She was not in the kitchen, though must have recently been so. I found one of her knives lying on the table amidst piles of half-chopped onions and potatoes. Although she had recently been preparing dinner, the door that leads to the pantry was shut. I never stopper my inkwell while I am using it; likewise Mrs Maguire never shuts the pantry door until the day is passed and gone. I grasped the doorknob, and even tried to twist it, but it slid loosely in my hand without turning. The knob was slick with blood. I did not dare to try and open the pantry again. My cassock is still stained with dried blood where I wiped my hand.

The stairs to the third storey came two and three at a time as I dashed up them. I could not climb them fast enough, and despite my deepest wishes, nothing discouraged or stopped me from continuing. The upper hallway was a void of darkness, and the same foetid odour that permeated the confessional filled the corridor like the blossom of a decaying flower. Having no source of light, I felt my way blindly down the hall. In my mind I recalled each of the paintings that hung in the hall as my fingertips brushed across them, until I knew that I stood before Fr Sheridan's door. I prayed that it would be locked.

I threw open the door to Fr Sheridan's room with the last ounce of rational courage in my bones. The scene revealed to me by the opening of this door was a grotesque vision worthy of Collin de Plancy.[58] Fr Sheridan was propped up on a pile of pillows in his sickbed. He was dressed in a white gown, made many shades whiter by his scarlet red face from which his eyes protruded. His jaw was thrust open, chin nearly touching his throat; his tongue twisted like a struggling pink grub. Our eyes met in the instant that I entered the room, and in that instant I saw the life pass from them. His rigid body, muscles still tense with surprise, collapsed against the pillows.

Around Fr Sheridan's bruised throat were wrapped hands that I had once known so well. They were attached to the outstretched arms of a murderer whose visage I knew with equal intimacy. Hunched over the body of Fr Sheridan, leering at me with two eager eyes, was a man whose countenance reflected the features of Fr Sheridan's face with shocking exactitude. Even now my disbelief in

---

[58] Jacques Auguste Collin de Plancy (1793–1887) is the author of *Dictionnaire Infernal*, a catalogue of demons and their positions in the hierarchy of Hell. The book was first published in Paris in 1818. The 1863 edition was famously illustrated with striking depictions of the demons. Father Corrigan was likely familiar with this book through Father Sheridan's extensive personal library.

this vision is fractured. It was as if Fr Sheridan merely slept beside a life-sized portrait of himself, but the truth was vastly less desirable. And had I not seen one murder the other, I would not have been able to say which was which.

Almost as if the room were constricting around it, the fiend wearing Fr Sheridan's face straightened to its full height and filled the room with its mass. It looked down on me with unflinching and malicious desire. Only I obstructed the way between the door and the great imp standing before me. Driven by reasons that I can no longer remember, I reached up and felt pinned to my breast the dried lavender that Fr Sheridan had given me. A strong breeze blew across the room. I now noticed that the bed-room window was wide-open, admitting all that accompanies an autumn chill. The next gust was even stronger. It scattered papers and flapped the drapery, knocking to the floor the vase of dried lavender that had been placed in front of the window. Dried remains of lavender blew about the room, disintegrating and crumbling in the wind.

In one swift movement Fr Sheridan – no, the thing that bore Fr Sheridan's *likeness* – leapt across the room to the window. I do not know if I can fully trust my vision, but I fancied this infernal creature was now smaller than it was in the preceding moment. Though I had not seen it alter itself in size, it perched comfortably on the windowsill like a feline, ready to spring through the open window. In these terrible seconds, now displayed like a portrait of masterful realism in my mind, the demon glanced at me over his shoulder. And for this instant, this one awful moment before it sprang through the open window, I swear that it was *my* own visage that I looked upon.

I uprooted my legs in time to see my brother land effortlessly in the courtyard a full three-storeys below. Without pause for recovery, I watched as the creature darted across Rathmines-road and disappear into the dark folds of Larkhill.[59] One moment he sprinted on two legs like a man, the next he loped like a beast on all fours.

I fled Fr Sheridan's room and the wind-stirred tempest of loose papers and dried lavender. My bed-room is my sanctuary, secure in the relative certainty of pen, paper and ink. The door is locked and I have moved my writing bureau against it. I do not know what fates have befallen Fr Meagher and Mrs Maguire, or indeed what has become of the world outside this room since that demon escaped into the night. The only thing that I can be sure of is the judgment that surely awaits my inaction.

Not fifteen minutes ago I heard the tell-tale signs of a presence in the presbytery. I know every floorboard that squeaks, every door hinge that creaks, and every stair the groans. Once I even thought I heard a light tapping on my door, beckoning me to answer. I know my brother will come back for me. And I know I must wait for him to return.

This is where Father Corrigan's diary ends. From the distance of 130 years we are limited in our observations to those contained within this subjective historical document. What Father Corrigan experienced was real, but we can never be sure to what extent or in what capacity. I believe it is best to leave the interpretation to the individual reader; suffice to say that this allows for a range of

---

[59]Larkhill describes Larkhill House and its surrounding property, at the corner of Rathmines Road and Military Road, a short distance from Mary Immaculate. Until 1890, when the Holy Ghost Fathers purchased the property to open a college, Larkhill House sat derelict with its garden densely overgrown. Today this garden is St Mary's College's neatly trimmed sporting ground.

analyses, some of which may, I hope, explore possibilities which today we might feel more inclined to disregard.

Many of the facts related to the later entries in Father Corrigan's diary are independently verifiable. We know, for example, that the Church of Mary Immaculate suffered a particularly tragic year in 1881. Newspaper obituaries list Fathers Whelan, Sheridan and Meagher as having passed away in this year, though none of their brief obituaries elaborate on the perfunctory details. Father Whelan died of an 'unfortunate and accidental drowning'; Father Sheridan 'died peacefully in his sleep'; and Father Meagher 'passed on to his reward after a lingering illness' on 6 November. Father Meagher's obituary does not so much as hint whether his death was in any way connected with the incidents recorded in the diary. Canon Mark Fricker, who edited *Father Corrigan's Diary* for publication in 1922, succeeded Meagher in January of 1882.

The sanitarium in Glendalough to which Father Corrigan was committed in 1881 is still in operation. With a letter of introduction from the current curate of Mary Immaculate, the stern head nurse wearing a perpetual frown allowed me limited access to Father Corrigan's archived records. I am afraid I must report that the afternoon was not very illuminating. Father Corrigan never uttered another word after the night of 4 November 1881, and his days as a diarist were over. With no next of kin, he was admitted to the sanitarium under the diagnosis of 'Dementia praecox with pronounced aphasia', which lasted until his death. The attending physician, Dr Martin Simatic, noted that Father Corrigan's general disposition could be ascertained from his limited facial reactions. Under normal circumstances he conveyed 'in their contortions, the appearance of one under the duress of terror'. The nursing staff quickly learned that Father Corrigan grew 'calm and relieved of his unsettled state' with the introduction of fresh lavender into his room. It seems that, for the most part, and while the season permitted, the nurses did this with regularity until his death on 12 October 1882.

Epilogue

People have lived – and died – on this parcel of land since its earliest inhabitants christened it with a name now long forgotten. During the intervening years, events both noble and ignoble occurred in the very places that we still tread. There should be little wonder that the neighbourhood which we today call Rathmines is like a vast house, forever haunted by its former residents. Those among you with sensitive temperaments will understand what I mean. We notice the details that most do not. We see the stories that others are unable or unwilling to read. For us, the streets of Rathmines are long, dim corridors, capable of leading us to lonely places that not even the glow of streetlamps or neon signs can make pleasant. The buildings that line the streets are themselves entities, unique in their moods and vitalities. Many contain certain rooms that are by nature unwelcoming, and we would do well not to enter them. To do so would cause our stomachs to flutter, and the shadowy corners that subsist within would prickle the hair on the backs of our necks with disquieting expectation. What are these shades that exist alongside us? All we can hope for is that we do not enter one of these places whose disposition is darker than our own.

I could continue with stories tonight well until we reach the end of the road, but the town hall clock tolls the small hours, and it is time I should get home. I hope you have enjoyed our time together as much as I have, and that one day we might meet again. There are many dark corners yet to explore, and you should not be afraid to wander on your own. William Hope Hodgson, editor of that strange manuscript published as *The House on the Borderland*, wrote in his introduction: 'The inner story must be uncovered, personally, by each reader, according to his ability and desire.' To this, I paraphrase what Molly Crowe once told me: 'Admire these stories, but do so from afar and with the awe and respect that they deserve. Remember, Rathmines does not entirely belong to us. We who inhabit its antique buildings and well-worn paths do so only temporarily. Those who built this neighbourhood are now gone, but those who etched their existence into the fabric of Rathmines, sometimes, still walk among us.'

Thank you for your pleasant company, and I hope that your stroll home goes easy and undisturbed.

Brian J. Showers
Rathmines, Dublin
March 2007

Bibliography

Ball, Francis Elrington, *A History of the County of Dublin*, six volumes (Alex Thom & Co. Ltd, Dublin, 1902–1920).

Bell, Peter, *Strange Tales of York and the east Riding of Yorkshire: being a collection of the strangest cases investigated by Colonel Roger W. Ogilvie-Forbes, President of the York Society for Psychical Research, 1965–1992* (unpublished, 2007).

Bennett, Douglas, *The Encyclopaedia of Dublin*, revised and expanded (Gill & Macmillan, Dublin, 2005).

Bews, Harrison, *Solved! The Mystery of the Irish Crown Jewels* (Third Eye Press, London, 2003).

Burton, Nathaniel, *Letters from Harold's Cross* (Carraig Books, Dublin, 1850).

Byrne, Patrick, *Irish Ghost Stories* (Mercier Press, Dublin, 1971).

Corrigan, Simon, *Father Corrigan's Diary* (Irish Classics, Dublin, 1972; first edition, Hanna & Sons, Dublin, 1922; manuscript diary in 52 volumes, 1858–1881, in Church of Mary Immaculate, Rathmines, Dublin (Presbytery Library).

Costello, Peter, *Dublin Churches* (Gill & Macmillan, Dublin, 1989).

Curtis, Joe, *Times, Chimes and Charms of Dublin* (Verge Books Ltd, Dublin, 1992).

Delaney, Ruth, *The Grand Canal of Ireland* (David & Charles, Newton Abbot, 1973).

Dickson, David (ed.), *The Gorgeous Mask: Dublin 1700–1850* (Trinity History Workshop, Dublin, 1987).

Dungan, Myles, *The Stealing of the Irish Crown Jewels: An Unsolved Crime* (Town House, Dublin, 2003).

Glass, I. S., *Victorian Telescope Makers: The Lives and Letters of Thomas and Howard Grubb* (Institute of Physics Publishing, Bristol, 1997).

Hesselius, Martin, *Aufsätze zu metaphysischer Medizin* (*Essays on Metaphysical Medicine*) (Verlag Jaeger und Walbrun, Heidelberg, 1794).

Hodgson, William Hope, *The House on the Borderland* (Chapman & Hall, London, 1908).

Huberty, R. M., *An Examination of Imbibed Alcohols; their Addictive qualities, Harmful natures, and Delusional effects* (Johnson Street Press, Manchester, 1892).

Joyce, James, *Ulysses* (Shakespeare and Company, Paris, 1922).

Joyce, Weston St John, *The Neighbourhood of Dublin: Its Topography, Antiquities and Historical Associations* (M. H. Gill & Son Ltd, Dublin, 1912).

Kelly, Deirdre, *Four Roads to Dublin: The History of Ranelagh, Rathmines and Leeson Street* (The O'Brien Press, Dublin, 1996).

Kennedy, Brian P., *Jack Butler Yeats 1871–1957* (The National Gallery of Ireland, Dublin, 1991).

Kilpatrick, Bernie, *Phantoms and Apparitions of South Dublin* (Moreseer Press, Dublin, 1971).

Kissane, Noel (compiler), *Historic Dublin Maps* (The National Library of Ireland, Dublin, 1988).

Le Fanu, Joseph Sheridan, *The Cock and the Anchor, being a Chronicle of Old Dublin City* (William Curry, Dublin, 1845).

— 'Ghost Stories of Chapelizod', *Madam Crowl's Ghost and Other Tales of Mystery* (G. Bell and Sons Ltd, London, 1923).

McCarthy, Denis, *Dublin Castle: At the Heart of Irish History*, second edition (Stationery Office, Dublin, 2004).

MacGregor, John James, *Guide Book of Dublin* (1821).

Malone, Aubrey, *Historic Pubs of Dublin* (New Island Books, Dublin, 2001).

O'Connell, Angela, *The Rathmines Township: A Chronology & Guide to Sources of Information* (Dublin Corporation Public Libraries, Dublin, 1998).

Ó Maitiú, Séamas, *Dublin's Suburban Towns, 1834–1930* (Four Courts Press, Dublin, 2003).

Pearson, Peter, *The Heart of Dublin: Resurgence of An Historic City* (The O'Brien Press, Dublin, 2004).

Stoker, Bram, *Dracula* (Archibald Constable and Co., London 1897).

Sweeney, Clair L., *The Rivers of Dublin* (Dublin Corporation, Dublin, 1991).

Thom's Dublin Street Directory (Alex Thom and Co. Ltd, Dublin, 1852–2007).

Venables, Stephen, *Curiosities and Wonderments of the City of Dublin and its Environs* (Hanna & Sons, Dublin, 1736).

The newspapers and periodicals consulted are too numerous to list here. Anyone seeking more information on a particular reference should be able to track down the relevant details from the dates and footnotes provided in the text.

About the Author

Brian J. Showers is originally from Madison, Wisconsin. He attended that fine city's university and graduated in 1999 with a degree in English Literature and Communication Arts. He has written short stories, articles and reviews for magazines such as *All Hallows*, *Supernatural Tales*, *Ghosts & Scholars*, *Le Fanu Studies* and *Rue Morgue*. His book, *Literary Walking Tours of Gothic Dublin*, was published in 2006. www.brianjshowers.com

About the Illustrator

Duane Spurlock has illustrated chapbooks for The Swan River Press and did interior illustrations for *Literary Walking Tours of Gothic Dublin*. He also maintains The Pulp Rack, a website which focuses on the popular fiction published in magazines during the first half of the twentieth century. He and his wife and their children live and garden, read and draw, and tell stories to one another in Kentucky. www.pulprack.com